SERENITY'S WARHEAD

A NOVEL BY

JOHN HEWITT

Pump Island Tales
Mill Valley, California

Other Novels by John Hewitt

Stranger in Baja (2005)

Under the Padre's Thumb (2012)

Drone Baloney (2014)

One Shoe (2015)

Reptile Wines (2016)

"This is Major Tom to Ground Control
I'm stepping through the door
And I'm floating in the most peculiar way
And the stars look very different today"
　　　　　　　—David Bowie *Space Oddity—*

Serenity's Warhead

First published June, 2018

For more information, go to the website:
johnhewittauthor.com

Or contact the author at:
jh@johnhewittauthor.com

ISBN-978-0-9995336-5-9

Cover and book design by Jim Shubin
www.bookalchemist.net

Printed in the United States of America.

For Jerry and Bill
Their ideas and encouragement

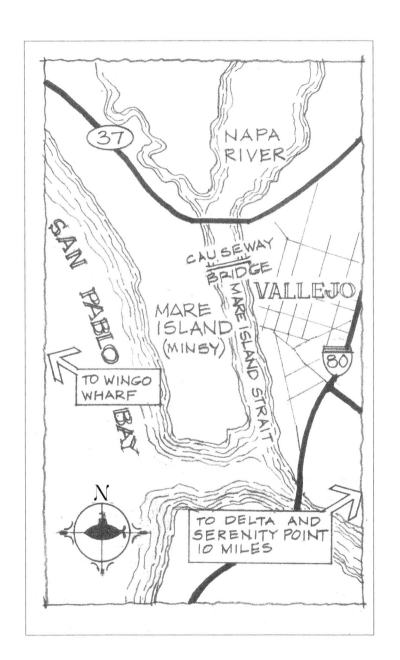

1
An Explosive Debut

On a brisk Saturday in October, shoreline surveillance video in the California port city of Vallejo captured a remarkable moment—Mitchell Wellborn's clumsy attempt to strangle his influential friend Coast Guard Lieutenant Commander Noah Merrydale.

Smack in the middle of a grandstand filled with cheering witnesses.

Then again, after what had happened earlier, who could blame Mitch?

The day started off on an upbeat note. Larger than expected crowds had arrived early to nail down choice seats in the Shoreline Park bleachers. They were bundled against the morning chill to see the city's decorated yacht parade, the traditional spectacle of pirate-themed boats that always kicked off the annual Vallejo Waterfest Weekend festival.

In the distance to the north, by the Causeway

Bridge, the contest boats circled, waiting for the cue to get in line.

Precisely at nine, two parachute flares shot into the sky, exploding in red starbursts. Air horns blatted out a fanfare. The festooned cruisers and sailboats began merging into a single file that would creep toward the reviewing stand.

The crowd stirred but seemed subdued.

Mitch fretted about their lack of enthusiasm. The mayor had chosen him at the last minute as the city's interim Waterfest manager. His orders were to make it a rousing success.

Or else.

As the procession neared, the spectators in the bleachers began to laugh. They were pointing to a smoke trail out on the water.

Mitch couldn't contain his curiosity. He had busted his ass to wheedle an impressive rescue vessel from the Coast Guard to lead today's pageant. But what he saw through his binoculars steamed him.

There was no long-promised silvery Coast Guard Motor Life Boat in sight. No forty-seven-foot high-tech surf-busting monster. Instead, the festival's Mermaid Queen Jaylyn Chadwick and her rented costume tail led the parade perched atop something that looked like a self-propelled six-foot-long garbage can skimming inches above a light chop of gray seas.

Diesel smoke billowed from beneath her.

She looked scared.

Mitch turned to his friend Commander Merrydale beside him in the VIP section. "Noah. I am not seeing your badass Coast Guard boat you swore would be here. Because it's obviously not here. And no one told me. Instead, there's this...this... little tube thingie... I don't know what it is... under my festival queen. What the hell gives?"

"Cutbacks."

"Cutbacks?"

"Yeah. The Guard nixed the big boat. But I found you a righteous replacement—this home built Colombian drug-running mini-sub we captured off Baja last week. It only runs underwater. We call it El Gordo."

"Look. Your superboat's picture is all over my program cover. Rah, rah, Coast Guard. Now there's this dipshit tube, like a horizontal water heater."

The Commander gave Mitch a moment to cool it. "Sorry I didn't tell you. But that water heater is the mini-sub's ingenious superstructure that stays above the surface. It's the only thing you can see and is an exhaust port for the diesel and fresh air for the crew. If our drug smugglers in El Gordo are caught in the open ocean, they jettison that cylinder by firing off plastic explosives, and then sink the crazy tuna-fish-shaped hull full of cocaine. Nifty?"

"Not really. Your Coast Guard Motor Life Boat is a lot flashier. And it floats, so it's visible. Visible. All the boat nuts on shore can see it. Yes. Seeeeee it."

"Sorry."

"Sorry. Sorry my ass. You've got your cushy Coast Guard career so this little ghost sub is no fuzz off your butt. On the other hand, Bucko, I stay employed if I make a success of this cruddy festival. The Mayor will be here in a minute. Right now, my assistant harbormaster job is on slippery footing. And unless my startup comes in with a windfall, I'll be selling hot dogs, scooping worms in the bait shop, running the fuel dock and cleaning marina bathrooms the rest of my life."

"Mitch. You know how the Guard can be. It was out of my hands. So, chill out. Besides, what else could go wrong?"

The yacht parade meandered down the center of the half-mile wide channel called the Mare Island Strait, the Napa River outflow where it spills across shoreline mudflats and into an arm of San Francisco Bay. This inland waterway, twenty miles north of San Francisco, separates the U.S. Navy's now abandoned Mare Island Naval Shipyard, known as MINSY, from the city of Vallejo.

Inside the cramped Colombian mini-sub, three hundred-pound Coast Guard Petty Officer Third Nelson was alone and frustrated by makeshift controls labeled in Spanish, a language he didn't speak. This was his first shot at driving this boat. His orders were to keep El Gordo on a course toward the reviewing stand.

Vallejo's Mayor Hope Stinger finally arrived at the bleachers, wedging herself in between Mitch and the Commander. She clutched her squirming ten-pound miniature terrier Chipper.

The Mayor grinned. "Mitch, I bet you've got a pocketful of doggie treats. You think the way to a woman's heart is through her pooch. But it's not. Never will be. That's your lesson for today. Still, Chipper loves you and he never forgets. Take him for me."

The dog jumped into Mitch's lap.

The Mayor made a gesture toward the sky. "Wow. We've got a beautiful morning. Blue skies. Puffy white clouds." She held up the festival program's cover. "And you scrounged up this snappy Coast Guard rescue boat I so love. Mitch, our military's sexy craft really show the rest of the world America's seagoing greatness. What a coup."

She reached out to Mitch. "Now, lend me those binocs, will ya?"

The Mayor scanned the channel. "Omigod. What's this? Where's my red-striped tug-boat-looking Coast Guard wonder boat? And what's this cloud of smoke in the channel? Your Mermaid Queen looks like she is freezing to death. All she's got on is some sort of body stocking with a coconut shell bra, a tiara and a giant fish tail. And tell me your Mermaid Queen is not riding a coal-burning jet-ski?"

"It's actually the tippy-top sail of our wonderful last minute substitute attraction, the Colombian drug smuggling mini-sub, El Gordo. Courtesy of your U.S. Coast Guard."

The Mayor had a pained look. "Mitch, I can't see it. Where is this El Gordo?"

"Underwater. Running deep."

"Can't you at least get them to putt-putt his stuff above the surface?"

"No, he wasn't designed to putt-putt topside. He's a semi-submersible. We never will see him."

"Why have something you can't see leading our parade? You've had four weeks to get this opening day right. And now a drug mule with all that foreign ugly smoke looks so cheap. I know the city council will rag on me for this."

"Well, Madame Mayor, in a few moments, I am going to murder my dear benefactor, the Coast Guard officer sitting beside you. I am sure this will be recorded on surveillance video. Show that to the council for excitement. The Guard screwed me over. Vallejo has been screwed over."

Mitch lunged toward Merrydale and got his hands around his throat before the Mayor pushed them apart. "Not now boys," she said.

At that moment, the crowd erupted in a roar. The festival's chartered 26-foot Boston Whaler with twin outboards was doing showy S-turns while making a noisy pass in front of the bleachers. This was the official media boat. Freelance photographer Maggie Trout stood on the bow, secure in a harness lashed to the steering podium, waving to the crowd.

The submerged El Gordo was mid-channel approaching the front of the judges reviewing stand. On Mitch's cue, the Vallejo High marching band struck up a dreadful off-key techno version of the Navy's Anchors Aweigh anthem.

The public address announcer did her best to whip up the crowd. "Now the moment we've been waiting for…the lead vessel in our Waterfest parade… provided by your U.S. Coast Guard…the advanced Motor Life Boat rescue ship 88666 Golden Gate. Stealth design. The bad guys will never see this coming. Your tax dollars built this million-dollar space age rig. Ain't she a beauty? And on its foredeck, our lovely festival sparkler, Jaylyn the Mermaid Queen. Give her a big welcome."

There was, of course, no fantastic boat. Just Jaylyn, a local Solano Community College sophomore, picking up extra pizza money playing the role of the Mermaid Queen while freezing atop a seagoing garbage can. The crowd applauded weakly.

The Commander shouted "No. Wrong. Stop this. Completely wrong."

Mitch groaned. He set Chipper on the ground.

Inside El Gordo, Nelson reached down for his coffee but his size sixteen uniform boots bumped a glowing red security lever marked "peligroso." A claxon loud enough to be heard on shore sounded with an "AH-OGG-GAH" alert.

Merrydale said "No. Oh God no. Now, he's done it. Mitch. Oh, shit. I think Nelson hit the kill switch that scuttles El Gordo."

Indeed. He had. That single misstep put the cartel built drug sub on an irreversible course—it was destined to sink itself—and Mitch's future—in less than a minute.

The shoreline audience could hear a muffled clunk

as two forward hatches sprung open, flooding the bow. Wafts of white steam began curling across the water from beneath the queen's garbage can perch.

Jaylyn panicked and stopped waving. The steam engulfed the queen and her mount. Mitch buried his face in his hands. "I'm dead. Dead," he kept repeating.

Then three loud pings, then the claxon again. Finally a thunderous blast of El Gordo's plastic explosives rocked the channel, sending out a billowing cloud of churning smoke.

The fiery concussion blasted Queen Jaylyn vertically from the surface, firing her into the blue like a rocket headed to the moon. As she soared higher, the gangly queen, with a goofy look on her face, her arms spread wide, her shock of black hair buffeting behind her, continued alone, tracing a shimmering arc across the sky, a fish-tailed cannonball on the ride of her life. Spectators guessed her ballistic trajectory reached a height of a three-story building before angling downward. The flight lasted only seconds, but seemed like an eternity.

Mitch watched transfixed, thinking *This is not happening*.

His Mermaid Queen, still wearing the expensive rented costume, splashed down fins first in a shallow stretch of the mucky Mare Island Strait ninety yards from El Gordo. She disappeared beneath the surface.

A huge cheer rose in the bleachers.

The announcer was delirious, shouting "What a show. VA-LAY-HO. Can you believe it? VA-LAY-HO.

Let's hear it for VA-LAY-HO." The crowd picked up the chant "VA-LAY-HO" and rhythmically pounded their feet on the wooden bleachers while whistling like drunken spectators at a strip club mud-wrestling match.

Lieutenant Commander Merrydale swallowed his gum. He also called 9-1-1.

The Mayor stood and applauded, yelling over the crowd noise. "Hey. Mitch. Everyone is really so into it. Loved the fireworks and the flying mermaid. Did you see the look on her face? Great acting. I'm impressed. So exciting. You made up for the AWOL sexy boat with a great show."

"Ms. Mayor. It's not a show."

"Say again," the Mayor said.

"That wasn't supposed to happen."

2
The Rescue

The Whaler media boat sped to the spot where Jaylyn had gone under. For still unexplained reasons, photographer Maggie Trout ducked out of her harness, set down her camera and jumped into the frigid, murky Strait.

Maggie dog-paddled over, reaching the mud-covered festival queen as she surfaced, gasping for air. "Help. Please help me."

The two thrashed and struggled before Jaylyn climbed onto her rescuer's shoulders, pushing her head under water. After an eternity, Maggie untangled herself from the Jaylyn's legs and resurfaced behind her. She fumbled in the water, grabbed the queen's costume tail and towed her back to the Whaler. The crew pulled them aboard.

Still chanting "VA-LAY-HO", the spectators stomped louder in a wild deranged frenzy. The high school band thundered ahead, supplanting skill with volume, as it murdered the iconic music.

Inside the doomed El Gordo, there was panic. Beefy Coast Guard driver Nelson was desperate for a way out. The explosion had blocked his getaway route through the main hatch. Seawater was filling the forward hull. He opened a rearward supply hatch and began to wiggle free, but his baggy uniform snagged on the latch. His struggle left the uniform behind. When he surfaced, he was buck-naked except for his spit-shined Coast Guard uniform boots and his yellow self-inflating life vest. He climbed onto the sinking deck of the mini-sub, steadied himself and gave the startled audience a full-frontal nude salute before diving into the murk in a frantic effort to escape.

Once more, the Whaler crew roared back to pluck Nelson from the frigid Straits. They tossed him a life-saving ring, then strained to maneuver him to the hull. His girth and slippery skin made hoisting him aboard impossible, so the photo crew lassoed his boots and began towing him feet-first back to the dock.

Unmanned, El Gordo chugged in erratic circles in mid-channel, its bow swamped. This forced the still buoyant stern to rise up like a pleasure seeking gray whale in heat. Soon the sub's tail had risen to a near vertical Titanic-like pose in front of the reviewing stand. There it paused, for what seemed like forever, before sliding, with a colossal "BLURP," out of sight on a death dive to the muddy bottom of the 25-foot deep channel.

Festival video crews on shore grabbed their gear and ran to the dock to meet the photo boat. The band's director brought down his baton and the music ended. The spectators, sensing a screw-up of major proportions, quieted to a funereal silence and looked over toward the mayor.

The Mayor turned to Mitch. "Will it come back up?"

"Don't think so," Mitch said. "Let's ask our Coast Guard. Hey, Commander Merrydale, is El Sinko coming back up?"

Merrydale sat with a weary look. "Not right away."

"When?" the Mayor demanded.

"Next week," mumbled the Commander. He avoided the Mayor's stare.

Her voice shot up an octave. Her eyes smoldered. "Next week?"

"Next week. Maybe."

Chipper looked up and growled. The Mayor's mood turned a shade ugly. "Commander. I represent the City of Vallejo and I officially request you get that douchebag drugmobile out of my channel. It's a menace to maritime commerce. And not next week. Do it so like today."

"Madame Mayor. You've got a sunken submarine on the seafloor, not some shitty little fiberglass pleasure cruiser. It's going to take serious salvage assets to refloat it. Tugs, cranes and barges. If there aren't any nearby, it might be weeks. I'll work this problem but can't guarantee anything."

"I want that thing out tonight. You blew it up. You get it out. I have friends in high places. I'll get journalists like Hunter Callahan of Fox News to screw with your career if you don't get this out so expeditiously."

"Keep your blouse on, Madame Mayor. Unless your favorite newsboy personality Callahan owns a handy barge, it's just not going to happen that fast. And by the way, don't you start blaming the Coast Guard for this mess. Your guy Mitch wanted something special for the parade. And I got it for him, but he just couldn't handle it. Tell that to your friend Hunter what's-his-name."

With his mobile phone glued to his ear, Merrydale slipped out of the bleachers and started jogging to the dock to meet the photo boat.

The Mayor turned to Mitch. Her eyes sparkled. "Wow. That Coast Guard Commander likes a good fight. In a perverse way, I get the shudders from my ankles when I talk with that guy. He's got command presence. You need to take lessons from a stud like him."

"From that double-crossing, uptight dipshit?"

"Yeah, and then you might actually be of use to a real woman."

"Said by a real woman who trolls the karaoke bars for dates."

"Yeah. So I like guys who can sing. Remember, your one-nighter with this mayor rated about a three on a scale of ten."

"Yeah, but you weren't the mayor then. Just the admiral's daughter."

"Or maybe that's because the cabin of your little boat stinks like dead fish and mold. And the bunks are too short and the sheets slimy. Honestly, I don't know how you convinced me to come back to the marina with you."

"If I remember, it was you who suggested it."

"Yeah, and I'll forever so regret it."

Mitch let it drop. He had the Waterfest to worry about and fallout was headed his way. The kickoff event had gone into the dumpster and his former friend, Mister Command Presence, had double-crossed him, ratting to the Mayor that Mitch's ineptitude was to blame for the fiasco. There still was the rest of the festival weekend, and that would feature the unique and first-ever in the world breaded-fish-stick-eating competition. That would show the chumps.

Right now, someone had to take charge. Mitch texted the parade monitors to send the yachts back to their marinas. He had security guards make sure the fire trucks and ambulances with blaring sirens could push through the crowd. The EMTs were sprinting along the shoreline on their way to meet the photo boat. Mitch followed them to the water's edge, arriving in time to watch the paramedics jump to the Whaler's deck and hand out thermal blankets to Maggie, the booted but still naked Coast Guard mini-sub driver Nelson, and the pathetic looking Mermaid Queen.

"What a mess," he kept mumbling, "gotta make the right moves now."

3

No Thanks

At the dock, the news mob was getting pushy. Jaylyn sat alone, shaking and exuding a stench of three-day old road kill. She stood to get ashore. Mitch saw an opening for a compassionate photo op, so he held his breath and reached out to steady her step to the seawall.

She pulled back her hand when she saw him.

"I'm really sorry," he said, as much for the reporters as for Jaylyn.

She ripped the tiara from her hair and threw it into the channel. "I can't hear a thing. Have to quit."

"You can't quit. What am I going to do? You are supposed to appear in an hour at the politician dunk tank."

The muddy queen narrowed her eyes to slits, and then hit her right ear with her closed fist. "Can't hear you. I'm deaf. Deaf. Understand. And I stink."

"Give it time," Mitch said. He turned to face the camera crews that had gathered. *A good moment to sound genuine* "Hearing always comes back. You know, my aunt lost her hearing playing the organ on

Sundays in church. But she got it right back." Then he turned back to Jaylyn. "Look, you did fine as queen. The best ever. People told me the spectators loved your waves."

"A lawn mower submarine. I'm smelly. And deaf. And I'm quitting."

"Look. Don't quit yet. If you walk out on me now, you'll pay for the very expensive costume tail you ruined and you won't get your salary."

Jaylyn exploded in fury and tackled the muscular Mitch like an enraged lioness taking down a sick eland. She ended up sitting on his chest, pounding her fists on his forehead. As she began to rub the slime from her hands onto his face, the paramedics intervened and hauled her off kicking and screaming to the ambulance, where they stretched her out on a gurney, wrapped her in warm blankets and roared off toward the Sutter Solano Medical Center.

He lay for a moment on the cement dock, trying to clear his eyes. The crowd had enjoyed the fracas, and the news reporters sniffed out a juicy tabloid backstory. Someone reached to help him up. Mitch dearly wanted to wipe the smelly gunk from his face but found himself standing in the open, facing a barrage of questions.

"Is the parade done with?" a reporter asked.

"Of course. It doesn't take brains to figure that out?"

"Chill out, Mitch. What about the rest of the festival?"

"I think it'll still go on. This afternoon, you guys shouldn't miss the fish stick Stuff-a-Thon. It's the first fried fish contest of its kind in the world."

"Will the queen be back for the Stuff-a-Thon?" A reporter asked.

"We'll have to wait and see. The doctors will decide."

"If she doesn't come back, are you really going to cancel her paycheck?"

Mitch forced a smile. "Look, guys, I was upset. Ok. The things I said. I was only kidding. Get it. Kidding. Of course she'll get her week's pay for being the Mermaid Queen. This whole thing. It's not her fault the mini-sub blew up. And it's not my fault either. The exploding mini-sub was the Coast Guard's fault. I had nada to do with it."

A reporter in the back yelled a question. "But you are ultimately in charge. Why is it the Coast Guard's fault that the thing blew up?"

"Because they low-balled Vallejo. Because they offered a cheap substitute. Because the Coast Guard doesn't give a dead squirrel about our Waterfest or our civic leaders."

Mitch was scrambling. "Let's go meet the hero," he said, steering the growing audience to where the photographer Maggie Trout sat on a short rock wall under a thermal blanket. She trembled and stunk like a corpse.

"Mags, very brave of you to jump in," Mitch said. "We all thank you for the gutsy rescue."

"My name is Maggie. Maggie Trout. I've told you that a hundred times, Wellborn. Calling me Mags assumes we have some sort of relationship. We don't."

A reporter shouted. "What made you jump in?"

"Jaylyn went under. I could smell fear. Someone had to act."

"Well, you saved the queen's life. That must make you proud?"

"I could have lost it. It's colder than icebergs out there. My heart almost stopped." Maggie stood up. "Look, I know you reporters are on deadline and I'll be happy to answer your questions another time. Right now, I'm tired and wet and smell awful so I want to get back to the marina to a warm shower. You all understand that. So, I need a little time."

Mitch wandered back. The Mayor watched his approach, frustrated by his blundering, wondering why the city's staff was burdened with such mediocre characters. She knew the man that she once interned for, and still dreamed about almost every night, Fox News's on-air personality Hunter Callahan, would have taken charge. He had command presence. He could show her the way.

Instead, she had to come up with a plan.

And she did. They didn't call her the "Monetizing Mayor" for nothing. "Mitch, despite your screw-up, our Vallejo will still come out ahead on this one. Jaylyn's flight and Maggie's water rescue are sensational stories. They'll intrigue social media users. I've already tweeted these and posted Instagram photos. Getting loads of hits. I've texted the vice-mayor to begin looking into copyrighting her flight. I'm going to make sure the city of Vallejo grabs all intellectual rights to Jaylyn's spectacular trip through the air. We can exploit the hell out of it. Sell movie rights. Toy submarines that look like El Gordo. T-shirts. Little Mermaid Queen dolls. Build a statue by the shoreline. Suck in tourists. Maybe get it on Fox News. I'll commission a local band to write a country song. Vallejo's citizens soon may so forget the Navy ever was here. This is going to be bigger than the usual story about a stupid lost whale trying to find a mate upriver. Jaylyn may become a moneymaker for the city."

Mitch studied the Mayor. Maybe she had gone off the rails. "Helluva bright idea, Mayor. Damned straight. A solid deal for the city. Waterfest will bring in truckloads of cash. Especially after this afternoon's fish stick Stuff-a-Thon."

The Mayor looked surprised. "Fish sticks?"

"Yeah. I cooked up this contest. Just a joke. Six contestants at a time try to stuff as many of these greasy fish sticks down their throats in a five-minute time period. This will be bigger than Coney Island's hot dog contest. No one, anywhere, has done fish sticks before. Vallejo will be the first. Ever. In the world."

"So, Mitch, tell me you can't screw this one up too," the Mayor said.

"How can I? It's perfect. And these locals pay a hefty entry fee to get into it."

"Well, I hope, for your sake, that it comes off all right. Also, I guess we should do some sort of city hall medal ceremony for the photographer lady who jumped in to save the queen—that Maggie person."

"Another excellent idea," Mitch said.

"This Tuesday night at the council. You organize it. And make it special."

"You're on."

"And don't forget to invite that hunky Commander buddy of yours."

Thus, Mitch Wellborn was entrusted with the role of matchmaker for his mayor and boss, a humiliating assignment for this man who had made a career of mediocrity as Vallejo's Assistant Harbormaster.

4

Medal of Disorder

The regular Tuesday meeting of the Vallejo City Council came two days later. It promised fireworks, but the hot topic wasn't the festival's exploding submarines or the fish stick medical disaster that followed—it was weed.

A vote to approve the operating license for a waterfront recreational marijuana processing plant, housed in an abandoned cement facility and backed by the BigWeed Consortium of Colorado, had muddied the air in Vallejo. The anti-plant coalition, Don't Smoke My Vallejo, filled half the seats in the chamber, ready to battle against this environmental ruin. The activists wore cardboard weed factory headbands and carried paddle signs that said "No Cannabis Hallucinogens". They expected a noisy protest would show the civic leaders there was deep-seated opposition to the plant.

BigWeed's backers had other ideas. Vallejo's business community as well as local construction unions had taken over the other half of the room with an equally boisterous mob.

The deeply divided crowd was ready for a confrontation. Signups for public comment speaker slots filled rapidly. City police and sheriff's deputies standing to the side watched with an uneasy feeling. The rage factor over airborne particulates had escalated to boiling. Any verbal fuss could set off a physical donnybrook, and then it would get very nasty.

To everyone's dismay, the BigWeed plant was the second agenda item. After the pledge of allegiance, councilwoman Louise Ortega-Khan called out her bitter political rival. "Mayor Stinger, during our normally sedate Waterfest, we had an exploding drug-smuggling submarine and five poisoned fish stick stuffers who went to the hospital on the city's nickel. And Vallejo looked ridiculous on the local teevee news. Please enlighten us how the Mayor's office didn't see this coming"

The Mayor straightened her shoulders. "I want to thank the council for this opportunity to tell you about how the city will benefit from all this."

"The last minute substitute lead boat for Saturday's yacht parade turned out to be a drug-smuggling Colombian mini-sub. The Coast Guard driver accidently activated a system that scuttled the vessel, using explosives to destroy itself before it sank."

Ortega-Khan interrupted. "Is it still there on the bottom of our channel?"

"Yes, but our Coast Guard is working furiously to get it raised. That was followed by Saturday's fish-stick debacle, something our disgraced Waterfest manager Mitchell Wellborn had concocted as a media-grabbing event, modeling it after the well-known Coney Island hot dog eating contest. Mister Wellborn unknowingly purchased knock off breaded fish sticks made, not from delicious American fish taken off the California coast, but from rancid fish parts imported from the polluted rivers of Myanmar. Because of Wellborn's pitiful ignorance, five Stuff-a-Thon contestants became violently ill and were taken to the Sutter Solano Medical Center where they had their stomachs pumped. But they are fine now."

The mayor also reported that the festival queen, Jaylyn Chadwick, was healthy again after spending a day and night in the hospital following the explosion of the mini-sub El Gordo. "At that point, with a view to the unfortunate events, our Waterfest impresario Mitch Wellborn graciously agreed to step aside. He will, however, retain his city job as Assistant Harbormaster, where he helps manage the bait shop and fuel dock at the Municipal Marina, although I might add, he will be on probation."

"You should note the bright spots in the Waterfest story. Attendance was up. Revenue from concessions, the gate, and parking was up. And, because we have obtained the intellectual property rights to the story of the Mermaid Queen's flight, Vallejo will rake in millions selling swag like sweatshirts, sub models, mermaid dolls, film options and script licenses," the Mayor said.

"Finally," she added with a smile, "to continue the celebration of our waterside heritage, in one month, November second, we will sponsor a mini-Waterfest called Re-Sail Fest. It will kick off with a mind-bending yacht parade."

Of course, all this drivel about the festival did nothing to calm the festering animosity between the marijuana plant protesters and partisans. The Don't Smoke My Vallejo advocates began a low chant, "no smoke" that was answered by the plant supporters who responded with "more jobs." That sparked chants of "drug fiends" from the anti-plant faction, which triggered re-chants of "kiss my ass, tree huggers." At one point, deputies rushed to staunch a shoving match and fistfight. They tossed the combatants from the chambers.

Hope banged the council's gavel and asked for consideration in the audience. The crowd quieted. "Vallejo is now going to recognize an amazing heroic deed by one of its citizens during the Waterfest. Maggie Trout, please come forward."

Maggie walked to the front of semi-circular council desk.

But there was more trouble in the crowd. Pushing and shoving erupted when someone grabbed a BigWeed factory sign and started batting it around the room as if it was a beach ball. Two men wrestled each other to the floor. Deputies grappled with the offending pair and hustled them to the exit.

"Please, I must have order. I must have order," the

Mayor begged. The crowd's arguments got louder. "Will you all shut up please," the Mayor yelled. A news photo of Maggie swimming appeared on an overhead screen behind the council desk. A second photo showed her struggling to pull Jaylyn to the boat.

"This is a special moment to recognize the heroism of one of Vallejo's longtime newswomen. I am speaking of Maggie Trout and her unselfish actions saving the Mermaid Queen during the opening parade for the Waterfest. Maggie, as we all know, has suffered a lot in the last few years. Laid off from the newspaper after twenty years as a staff shooter, she was sitting unsuspectingly in the front row when her ex-husband Rusty, our city's charming and lovable Recycling Manager, announced at the Vallejo Yacht Club Christmas dinner that he was dumping her to take up with a lithe and hot-looking nineteen-year-old bimbo aromatherapist in American Canyon. So, abandoned and alone, she had to begin life as an ambulance chasing paparazzi photographer while living alone on a moldy old boat in the marina. I mean, I don't know how she keeps it together and still has enough left in the old tank to save a drowning festival queen. Anyhow, Vallejo's Assistant Harbormaster Mitchell Wellborn has asked to read the council's proclamation."

The audience stilled.

Maggie stood alone in front of the council. Mitch carried his guitar to the speaker's podium at the left of the council's desk. He held the framed proclamation in his hands and started to read…"Be it known that on this day…whereas the Vallejo City council…whereas…whereas." He stopped and made a theatrical motion to drop it. "I can't read this. It's just a bunch of whereases and baloney. It's blah, blah."

Instead, he picked up his guitar. "I think her story is worth a song. It'll brighten the spirits here. I'll sing the real deal for you. I wrote this little ballad last night. I call it A Brave Woman Jumps Into the Muck." He played the iconic first notes of the Beatles song *Let it Be* on his guitar, and then sang in a nasal monotone.

> "She's so brave. She is the top.
> When duty called, she dove into the slop.
> Who else could save the Mermaid Queen
>   from certain death?
> It's all the Coast Guard's fault, that's for sure
>   we are to see."
> "Blame it on the Coast Guard…Don't blame
>   it on me."

The audience was restless. Hope rolled her eyes and pounded with the gavel. "That's enough, Mr. Wellborn, thank you."

But Mitch continued.

> "Maggie the brave…swam to the Queen …
> In icy water with an oil spill sheen…"
> She towed her tail to the City's Whaler,
> Another example of a Coast Guard failure.

The crowd booed.

Hope cut off the P.A. system. "Mitchell, get the hell out," she screamed. Mitch stopped singing and sat motionless, cradling his guitar.

All eyes waited for Maggie to react. The interlude of silence was double humiliation. Someone needed to take the focus off Maggie. Finally, a sympathetic environmentalist chose that moment to fire up a giant marijuana joint and blow the fragrant smoke into the air conditioning ducts. It billowed out in a sweet unmistakable cloud, triggering more shoving. New fistfights started. Deputies waded in with nightsticks.

The Mayor returned behind the council desk and stared out at the chaos, unsure of what to do.

That's when she spotted Lieutenant Commander Merrydale, in his Coast Guard dress blue uniform, standing at attention in the back of the room. He smiled at her and drew his finger across his throat.

Message delivered. Good advice. She acknowledged him with a smile, spread her hands out open to the ceiling, and shrugged. "I guess we have reached an intermission," she said, pounding the gavel. "With the council's permission, I ask the deputies to clear the room."

5

Maggie's Pistol Appears

The next morning, the rising sun struggled to burn through a gauzy overcast covering the Vallejo Municipal Marina. Chill breezes banged out the familiar rhythms of sailboat rigging clattering against the metal masts.

Maggie lay half-awake in the bunk on her boat, re-named the *Angry Duck* after her ex split. She listened intently to footsteps crossing the dock behind the cruiser. Suspicious characters and boat burglaries had picked up in the last few months. Maggie slid to the floor, pulled on baggy sweats, grabbed her loaded Ruger .44 Special revolver and hunched near the cabin door, ready for anything. The intruder continued along the floating dock, paused and then the *Angry Duck* rocked from side to side as a shrouded figure stepped onto the back deck.

Maggie burst out the cabin door and came face-to-face with a tall thin prowler in a black running suit with a hoodie.

"Stop right there," she screamed, holding the pistol in both hands and pointing the snub-nosed weapon at the invader's chest.

There was a smell of citrus. The suspect froze. The standoff was terrifying. "Maggie. Don't shoot. It's me. Jaylyn. From the festival."

Maggie lowered the gun. "Jaylyn. Shit. I might have messed you up. There have been nasty burglaries around here. I thought you were breaking in." She set the revolver on a sideboard. "How are you doing? How's the hearing?"

"Hearing is back. Mostly. But I am having trouble shaking the smell and I get throbbing headaches and all my bones ache. Still, I'm all right. I think."

"You got away lucky. You could have been blown to bits," Maggie said.

"Well, I'm glad that didn't happen. But something else weird is going on." Jaylyn paused. "Can we talk?"

"Come on in. Let me get you a cup of java? There's some already brewed."

"That's fine. I'd love some."

Maggie zapped two cups of coffee in the microwave. The women sat across from each other at the folding settee table. "So, Jaylyn, what's up?"

"I want to thank you again. It was so cool that you saved me."

"Enough said. You can jump in to save me sometime," Maggie said.

"No, really, it was awesome. I owe you. I mean, I beat you up out there."

"I survived."

"Wow." Jaylyn touched Maggie's hand. "Anyhow, I need your wise advice. Since that explosion, I'm jumpy. Every little noise is a trigger. And I have half-awake dreams. It's always the same one. I'm riding on that stupid Mermaid tube thingie. It explodes, and I'm blasting up from the water and soaring through the air with my arms spread out. And every time this happens, I get this pulsating feeling, and I begin to shudder. A warm pleasure jolt tightens my muscles, and then flows up through my body from my toes. My thighs vibrate. I begin to sweat and then I'm writhing and it detonates into a wild and happy ending. It's so hot. So joyful. It's the best ever. Then, I'm ravenous. I crave red meat. I want a steak."

Maggie was very interested. "You're kidding. Rapture? Then you want steak?"

"Rapture. Not kidding. Delicious. Intense. It's exhausting."

"This is weird to ask, but is it as intense as everyday sex?" Maggie said.

"You mean, like with a partner? No, this flying solo is so, so much better. The stuff with someone else can be a lot of work. Fiddling around with sweaty parts. Arms in the way. No, this explosive thing just happens. It sneaks up on me and then, wham. And it's far more satisfying than what I do myself. You know, with the mini-vibe."

"Well. Amazing. Don't know what to say. Maybe we should all get blown up."

"Yeah. The feeling is... so atomic bomb. And it happens three or four times a night. In the mornings, I'm wasted. But here's the dilemma. My neurologist at the Medical Center said that the explosive concussion has temporarily rearranged my neural connections in my brain, but that this condition will go away in a month or so. You know, return to dull old normal."

"Well, that's a relief,"

"No. No, Maggie. Wrong. Big wrong. I'd love to keep this going. I want to dream and enjoy the rides. So, here's the deal. Please don't tell anyone. I'm trying to find a way to recreate the situation. You know, like, get involved with another explosion? So, do you have any ideas about where I can find dynamite? Something that would launch me into the sky. I'm guessing it would have to be the whole package, the smoke and smells. I can't believe I'm asking for this. It's dangerous."

Maggie cocked her head. "No. That's way beyond me. But I'll look around."

"And to think I entered this silly festival queen contest during semester break to get scholarship money to pay the tuition."

"By the way, did that doofus Wellborn cancel your paycheck?"

"No. I think he was embarrassed. I got double the dough. Anyhow, soon I'm to meet with the mayor. She came to see me in the hospital the day after the explosion. My brain was still fuzzy and all I remembered was she wanted me to sign a pile of papers acknowledging the city's ownership of the copyright to my flight."

"And did you sign anything?"

"I think so. I was so out of it, I can't remember."

"What the hell? You're kidding. I don't understand

what she is copyrighting. She can't do that."

"Well, she says she has. And I'm not remembering what she said, but she talked about Vallejo having the rights to the story if movie companies start bidding on it. And, she has copyrighted my name. She says I can't even use my name."

"Your name? That's bizarre."

Heavier footsteps sounded on the dock. Maggie put finger to her lips. She edged to the window and peered through the curtains. This time, Mitch was standing on the stern, watch cap pulled down over his ears, his sandy hair sticking our by his collar. He was taking a picture of her cabin door with his phone. She rushed out holding the Ruger pointed in his direction.

Mitch raised his hands. "Whoa, Mags. Take it easy. I'm just shooting the silt underneath your boat. No need for a six-shooter"

"Mitch. You're looking at a five-shooter. Stop the bullshit about the silt. Take another fucking picture of me inside my cabin and you'll find out which one of the five has your name on it. This is assault, in case you didn't know."

"Please stop pointing that gun at me," Mitch said.

Maggie set the Ruger down. "You know, you're a friendly guy with passable qualities. But then you do absolutely thoughtless bullshit. Humiliating me at the council? What fucking reason did you have to sing that crappy song?"

"I thought it would be more personal than reading a dumb proclamation."

"Don't you ever stop to think that what you do might hurt someone?"

"It seemed like a good idea," Mitch said.

"Yeah, like a certain fish-stick eating disaster."

"Everyone knows the fish sticks got me fired from the Waterfest. Humiliated and escorted off the premises by the Mayor's royal security thugs after she went postal. Right now, I'm wearing my assistant harbormaster hat. That's why I'm shooting survey pictures for the dredging this week."

"You can't see the mud under my boat by peeping through my cabin windows. Face it. I say you are stalking me."

"Look. I'm doing this silt assignment. Just trying to get by until my Findola Tabs GPS startup gets sold to some bigger tech outfit for millions. Meantime, I spend my time here, there, and at the gym. And the gym has paid off. Check these out." Mitch raised his shirt and thumped his stomach. "Abs of steel, Mags." Another punch. "Women usually love this stuff."

"Not this woman."

"Maggie, you're trying too hard to fight it. I know you know that I'm far less of a jerk than your two-timing aroma chasing ex—Rusty."

"Look, Mitch. I don't start relationships by choosing the lesser candidate. Now, I've got a visitor. Good luck with the mud shots."

"No, think about it. Rusty always told me you were getting fat. I'm happy with women who have a little meat on their bones. That skinny little scarecrow therapist Tiffany would never turn my head. I can offer a lot, Maggie."

"Mitch. You don't know how stupid that sounds. Just shut up."

"Anyhow, you'll have to have the *Angry Duck* out of here by tomorrow mas rapido. We've offered you a temp covered slip on B dock but you never responded. I am assuming you will be off to that sordid gunk-hole marina you go to in the Delta?"

"I am taking the *Duck* out there. It's quiet and peaceful."

"Off to see a lover? Good luck getting a little bunkie buckaroo."

"Grow up, Mitch. I can't believe you said that."

"I'll put that down as a no comment."

Maggie ignored him. "Seen my dock neighbor Carver this morning? Is he on his *Doublecross*?"

"Five minutes ago, as the sun rose, Captain Fascist stumbled up the dock for breakfast."

Maggie returned to the *Duck's* cabin. "Jaylyn. I'm heading ashore to *The Sardine Can*, the local coffee shop for us live-aboards. Why not come along?"

"The what can? Where'd the place get that awful name?"

"I don't know. It's just been there forever."

"If it's okay, I'd rather rest. Maybe the boat's rocking will put me to sleep. You go."

In the crowded cafe, Carver Pardon sat alone at a window table. Even backlit, it was hard to mistake his bulky, round-shouldered body, thinning greasy hair, bulbous nose, and thick, drooping jowls. The former FBI agent, now retired, had been Maggie's next-door neighbor on the docks for two years.

Politically to the right of Attila the Hun, he was an intolerant character, always set to argue about anything political. Still, he and Maggie would nod hello. Dock mates with an uneasy truce.

She walked over. He grabbed onto her arm. The hair on his wrist had turned white and his skin was encrusted with blood bruises. His hand felt dry, like paper. "Look, I saw the video of the rescue on Saturday. You need to work on your freestyle swimming."

"Carver. Wasn't that stupid? I almost died."

"Stupid thing to do—jumping in. In that water. I'd never have done it, but I am sure that queen what's her name appreciated it. That took major cojones."

"Ovaries."

Carver relaxed his grip. "Are you shooting when they hoist the mini-sub wreck from the channel bottom?"

"I'm planning on it. I hired Erick's Zodiac. Not that you should care."

"Get me close-up pics. I'm an old submariner and would love to see what a drug cartel cooks up. I bet it's pretty unique. Tell you what. A pack of glossies and I'll owe you," Carver said.

"Owe me? What could I ever collect from you?"

"There may be a time. I do hear about photo shoot gigs. In fact, I know of one coming up. Pays good too."

"I'll think about it."

6

The Beast on the Bottom

Lieutenant Commander Noah Merrydale was a trim, short, balding officer with an athletic build, an insatiable love of boating and a lifetime career in the Coast Guard. He was ambitious, organized, followed regulations, and hated whiners. Because the blame for El Gordo's sinking landed on him, he feared reprimands, and maybe a demotion, an unfortunate move that would eviscerate the monthly retirement pension he hoped to start next year. However, if he handled this sub-raising in a smart fashion, it might take the sting out of the El Gordo affair.

By calling in favors owed by a few maritime salvage firms, it only took him three days to line up a crane and barge mammoth enough to re-float and haul away the sunken El Gordo. He tweeted the news editors they would be raising El Gordo tomorrow, a fast-tracked schedule he hoped would pacify the blood-sucking local media jackals that had hounded him daily.

An army of journalists swarmed to Vallejo. Calling this all-out team coverage, they took over every vantage point with their tripods. Crews filled parking lots with satellite trucks, laid miles of cable for lights and built small plywood risers for their reporters to do live shots. Then they gathered in the Mare Island Brewing Company to drink hoppy craft beer and commiserate about being stuck overnight in Vallejo. Boat charters were in high demand. Six photo crews hired local captains to take them to locations close to El Gordo's resting place. Maggie would hitch a ride on a zodiac inflatable.

In the morning, Merrydale was to be the Coast Guard front man for the first news conference. He showed up promptly at nine a.m., in a dress blue uniform. The crews had filled the ferryboat terminal lobby and cafe. It was standing room only when the television lights came on. CNN was beaming this live around the world.

"Good morning. I am Lieutenant Commander Noah Merrydale. I'm the officer in charge of the salvage operation. We have a barge over the wreck and we have private contract divers to work on it. We expect to finish in one day. We'll lift the mini-sub to the surface, pump it out, swing it onto a barge and take it to a dry-dock for inspection. You know, this mini-submersible is really a very exotic vessel."

Someone from the crowd interrupted, shouting "It's crap. It's no better than turtle poop. Why don't you tell them it's a piece of shit? And that's why it sank."

The glare from the camera lights blinded the Commander and made it impossible to see who was yelling. Finally, he spotted his former buddy Mitch Wellborn ten feet away, blue watch cap pulled down over his ears and face red with fury. The journalists' camera lenses zoomed in on his rage. He was ranting. "Yeah, Commander, why don't you tell them whose fault it was that El Sinko sank? Who else? The imperial Coast Guard. That drug bucket should never have been out there."

Merrydale rubbed his eyes. "Mitch. What's your problem?"

"Well, I was fired. Publically humiliated. During the tainted fish-stick-eating challenge. Okay, I admit it. Contestants got sick. How was I to know there were bones in the fish sticks? That they were rancid? Toxic? But the Mayor blamed me... me... for that fiasco and for your mini-sub explosion and so her security goons boxed up my goodies and escorted me off the premises."

"I'm sorry to hear you lost your job. As far as the sub goes, we haven't even begun an accident investigation. So, you'll just have to wait for that."

"Yeah, and if you run it, it's like the fox investigating the pig house. It'll mean more lies." Mitch was on a roll. "You caused it. You did. You military Pinocchio. Your fault. Liar."

Two thickset Coast Guardsmen in dark blue moved to stand in front of Mitch. They tried to calm him. He pushed them away. "Get your hands off me, you imperial goons."

The duo began to herd him toward an exit. Mitch was not cooperating. A wrestling match broke out before the huskier Guardsman grabbed him in a headlock and then shoved him through a side door and into a hallway. Everyone could hear a great deal of banging and scuffling in the corridor. Mitch kept up his tirade offstage. "You won't get rid of me this easy. I'll haunt you fakers everywhere. Pinocchio liar."

Once the fracas quieted, the Commander scanned the room and addressed the reporters. "Sorry about the interruption."

A reporter asked, "Is this sub raising a routine job?"

"Not really. Visibility stinks. You can only see about four feet, even with lights. We are a bit lucky— it's upright on the bottom. But we're dealing with an inert vessel whose screw is half-buried in the slimy channel muck. Also, it's a homebuilt, and we have no blueprints, so we don't know the stress points on the hull. Also, this beast is full of seawater."

"What's your first step?" The reporter asked.

"The divers need to survey the exterior for obvious hull damage. Then, we'll fit straps into a harness at both ends before attaching inflatable pods. At the same time, we'll prep the hatches and get ready to pump out the seawater once we can bring it to the surface. That should take six hours."

"Once it's on the barge, where does it go?"

"To Coast Guard station Alameda. Then we'll decide what to do with it."

Then the question he didn't want. "How much is this fiasco costing the Coast Guard?"

"Fiasco is your word. We don't consider this a fiasco. We haven't totaled up the cost yet, but it isn't cheap to raise a sunken submersible. And we don't know who will pay for it," the Commander said.

Merrydale scanned the room. "Okay, if no more questions, I want to introduce Vallejo's mayor, the Honorable Hope Stinger, who has a few words."

There were snickers as the stylish city leader, wearing a blue Vallejo Yacht Club blazer and cradling her snarling Chipper in her arms, strode to the mic. She flashed a radiant smile, set the pooch down, turned sideways and took Commander Merrydale's hands in both of hers. It was a photo op handshake. "Thanks so much for your service," she said loud enough for all to hear. She also slipped her business card with her personal home phone number into his uniform pocket.

"Hello and thanks to all of you for visiting Vallejo to cover our first city sponsored Vallejo Sub-Raising Festival. I am Mayor Hope Stinger and I invite you all to partake in the delights of our local cafes and bistros when you need to sustain your energies. We have two craft breweries, one in this very building."

The reporters hooted at the mention of breweries.

"First some background. I know you all were taken with the story of Jaylyn Chadwick and her Mermaid's Flight—now a standout moment in Vallejo's storied history—and part of the American dream. But I must inform you that the City of Vallejo has copyrighted the video of Ms. Chadwick's journey through the air last Saturday. Therefore, you cannot replay it without a release from the city. You also cannot use her name, Jaylyn, which we have trade-marked. However, you can obtain a license to do that by paying a small fee to our city controller who is sitting at a fold-up portable table by the door. Any questions on that part?"

One of the local TV reporters jumped up. "You're kidding?"

"Not kidding."

"You want us to pay you to use what you call your news?"

"You'll have to respect our copyright. It's the law. And yes, you'll have to pay," the Mayor said.

"Look. You cannot copyright anything that was visible from a public place and that was already shot. We have every right to use it."

"Not unless you want to go to court. You didn't shoot it. Our hired crew shot it. It's ours. We have watermarked the video, and inserted graphics that tell of our ownership. We will vigorously prosecute any violators of our copyright."

"This is going to put a chilling effect on the First Amendment."

"Look, don't be a whiner about this trivial amount. Man up. All you have to do is pay the dinky user li-cense fee and you can show it until your eyeballs drop out."

"Well, it does bring up freedom of the press questions."

"Oh, for god sakes, just pay. It's no big deal. Vallejo needs the money," the Mayor said. "And this brings me to our second topic—the inexpensive paid press access for today's First Annual Vallejo Sub Raising Festival. Because this event is a city-sponsored happening, we are allowed to charge access fees to your video teams. Credentials come in stages. If you buy the blue access, we welcome your photography from locations along the shoreline. Purchase the more expensive yellow credentials and you will be allowed to shoot or photograph the event from a boat or a helicopter, but you must stay at least a half-mile from the salvage barge. The next access is called the red zone, which gets you up close and personal, at least a quarter mile away. Finally, there's our own pool photographer at ground zero, and if you wish to purchase a license to use this pool footage or any of our stills, then pay our controller for the gold pass at the door."

There was outrage. A few news crews displayed the middle finger salute for the Mayor. Others stood and threw wadded up copies of the press release.

A reporter yelled. "Isn't this a news event involving the United States Coast Guard?"

"Yes," said the Mayor, "but it is happening on city land, albeit under water. The submarine rests within our city limits. Therefore, we can legally sponsor a festive event, and control access by the public. Historically, municipalities have been allowed to charge a reasonable fee for access. You guys can purchase the credentials with the city staff at the pop-up table by the door."

"This is more horseshit," yelled another reporter. The crowd picked up the chant. "More horseshit.

More horseshit." A blizzard of crumpled press releases peppered the front of the room.

"Look. Just play along," the Mayor yelled over the
din. "And give this note to your assignment editors.
Vallejo will restage the yacht parade in one month,
on November Second. This event will be called The
Re-Sail Fest."

She reset the microphone on its stand and smiled.
The Commander was standing at her side, shoulders
back and beaming. He grinned and gave her the
thumbs up.

Hope decided then and there that it was command
presence that put the wind in her sails.

The moment had arrived for Hope's second test
for the Commander. Somehow, she had to get him
to a karaoke bar. This was vital to her experience—
her partners had to sing.

7

The End of the Line

For most of Wednesday, the salvage operation was routine. Air pumps on the barge hissed at regular intervals. Divers came and went with cables and inflatable pods. At four in the afternoon, with the short October day drifting into twilight, the divers surfaced and motioned to pull it up. The powerful winches on the salvage barge groaned as the cables tightened. The media boats with red credentials circled where the cables entered the water, waiting for something, anything, to happen.

The silvery bow of El Gordo's tuna fish shape was the first to break the surface, dripping water as it rose into view. Ever so slowly, more of the metal hull emerged. Streaming video feeds allowed viewers around the world to watch the revealing moment. Once the main hatch rose above the waterline, crews installed pumps to evacuate the seawater. Minutes later, the El Gordo's stern popped above the surface.

Everyone froze.

Commander Merrydale's voice crackled over the walkie-talkies. "What is it? What's the holdup?"

"There's a lot of tension on the stern. We've got a line around the screw and it's hooked to something heavy. We're pulling up junk off the bottom."

The crane operators slowed the winch's speed, tightening the aft harness inch by inch. A puzzling twelve-foot-long tube emerged at the end of the cable. The machinery stopped once the mystery piece dangled inches above the water's surface.

The tube had the diameter of a torpedo and was covered with mud. Both ends were blunted.

A Coast Guard boat with the Commander circled the mystery dangler. He grabbed his radio. "Set a security perimeter." Maggie had lucked out. Her zodiac charter was closest to the mysterious object. She managed to shoot over thirty stills before Navy launches blockaded the area and herded all civilian boats away. Coast Guard choppers flew above the photography charters and used loudspeakers to turn them back. The news helicopters were sent packing. Navy personnel on shore pushed spectators toward the parking lot.

To the experienced eye, the derelict hanging off El Gordo's screw had to be a torpedo—at least half of it. Yet it had an odd, two-stage design, like two different diameter pipes joined together. One end was sheared off, as if a nosecone was missing.

The discovery energized Vallejo, a Navy town chock full of retired officers and crews. A derelict weapon pulled from the muddy channel bottom stirred more speculation than if an alien had landed

at the ferry terminal. This waterway had been the entrance to a U.S. Navy submarine base during WWII
and the shipyard had built twenty-nine nuclear submarines here in the days of the Cold War. A single
vagrant torpedo dredged to the surface would not
be a surprise.

The retired chief petty officer piloting Maggie's zodiac had served on a nuclear-powered attack submarine. As they sped away, he enlightened Maggie. "It's
the body of one of those nuke-tipped fish. Called a
44. A SUBROC. Get it? SUB ROC, short for submarine rocket. The boats carried these in the seventies.
But it looks like this one has no warhead. It's been
disarmed."

The mystery weapon's outline, streamed live
on CNN, ignited a flurry on the Internet. Opportunistic
conspiracy theorists sprang into action, inundating
Facebook and YouTube. Wild guesses suggested this
was one of ours or a Soviet surveillance torpedo
buried in the mud and left over from the Cold War.

The Coast Guard had been caught flatfooted. Now,
they huddled on how to put this cat back in the bag.
They brought in the Navy, whose sailors installed
tarps to shroud the unexpected visitor. Three hulking
U.S. Navy Sea Knight helicopters, turbines whistling,
arrived on the shoreline. The military said nothing
and scheduled a news conference that night at the
Vallejo ferry terminal.

Roving units approached photojournalists and demanded their pictures. They huffed and puffed about
"national security." Maggie's zodiac charter pulled

up at the Vallejo Municipal Marina D dock just as two thick-necked buzz-cut Navy officers arrived. They ordered her to hand over the camera. She refused. One grabbed her Nikon and pulled out the memory card. He pocketed the storage device and then handed the expensive Nikon back to her.

Maggie said, "You can't do that."

"It's a national security issue. File a claim for the card. They'll pay you."

The sullen duo left with the card.

A quick inspection determined that the camera wasn't damaged. She scrolled through the onboard storage of the pictures she had taken. She still had them. The Navy goons didn't know that this Nikon model backed up the memory card with an internal storage that contained the last thirty shots.

Maggie dashed into the *Angry Duck* and transferred the pictures onto a flash drive. The valuable Nikon went into a false wooden panel overhead the cabin settee and table. She grabbed another camera kit and hitched a ride along the shore to the news conference.

That evening, the building was jammed when the Commander stepped up to the microphones. "Once again, I am Lieutenant Commander Noah Merrydale of the U. S. Coast Guard. Thank you for your cooperation with our crews. You all are now aware that the unexpected has happened. If we have seemed pushy at times, it is because what we dredged up might be a dangerous weapon. We don't know how old it is or how unstable it is. Don't know if it is carrying explosives or volatile solid fuel propellant and if these are still dangerous. Therefore, we are keeping everyone at least a half-mile away. We appreciate your cooperation with our security perimeter."

A reporter yelled. "Is it that submarine rocket called a SUBROC?"

"We can't say yet."

"There is speculation by reliable Internet weapons specialists who are saying that this might be a Soviet surveillance device. So my question is: Is it theirs?"

"Don't know who these Internet weapons specialists are. We are still investigating," the Commander said.

"In the last hour, I've read that experts from the former Soviet Union say that the Soviets copied our design for the underwater sub-killing SUBROC, and turned it into a listening post to monitor sub traffic in the channel."

"Sorry. As I've said, I haven't any information on Soviet weapons."

"But it could be a leftover Soviet…"

"No info. Asked and answered. Let's move on," the Commander said.

"So are you denying the connection to the old Soviet military?"

"There is no evidence of any old Soviet involvement."

"If it still has a warhead, what will you do?"

"We'll take it to the appropriate facility and disarm it."

"Even if it was a nuclear one?"

"That will have to be determined." The Commander

shrugged. "These things take time. I'd like to be able to tell you more but our primary concern is to determine the explosive danger it might have. We'll have more in the morning."

There was a shout from the left. "Tell them, Merrydale, about how your incompetent Coastie scuttled the mini-sub. Yeah, your fault. Not mine. Then tell the Mayor."

Mitch Wellborn was in the back of the room, his blue watch cap still pulled down over his ears.

"Mitch, you should go home before you get into trouble. Again."

"No, Pinocchio, tell the media. Tell them how your ignorance sank it. You didn't want anyone to know how inept the Puddle Police is. Today you pulled up something that could embarrass the Navy top brass. Maybe, just maybe, this was the work of the rumored super secret Trap Door rogue scientists. And if you can't explain that, there goes your rank and retirement. At least I hope so."

"Don't know what you mean by Trap Door," the Commander said.

"Oh. Come on. Don't play dumb. Everyone in Vallejo knows Trap Door was a cold war rogue operation in the shipyard that spooked the Navy."

"Sorry. Can't say."

Mitch continued to sputter but the Commander was done with questions. He turned from the podium and walked away from the microphones.

8

Another View

"Excuse me."

"Behind ya."

"Pardon me."

The Commander pushed through the milling news crowd. His second public tiff with Mitch had been frustrating. *What could he do to stop that nutcase and his confrontations? Why did Mitch bring up that Trap Door conspiracy fable about a group of rogue scientists with their own atomic secrets?* Merrydale thought that bogus secret cabal nonsense had been debunked long ago.

The last person the Commander bumped into before escaping out the exit was Carver Pardon, Maggie's antagonistic marina neighbor.

Carver pushed back.

Carver was both giddy and worried. Mitch's public resurrection of the Trap Door conspiracy theory thrilled him. Carver invented that fable years ago to throw people off the trail of the real Mare Island security problems. Now Trap Door would once again confuse the public's curiosity.

But today's official explanation of the dangling weapon was worrisome. This was not a simple case about finding a genuine long lost fish. He needed to see it.

Carver was in a unique position to be concerned. His career, as he explained on his website, began as a graduate of the Naval Academy at Annapolis, and that led to tours on submarines. Next, a switch to security at the Mare Island Shipyard, spending a decade chasing down leaks of classified information. He resigned his commission to take a job with the FBI and then the NSA in Washington, where he headed a task force specializing in foreign espionage.

Left off his official bio were the growing concerns about his fading memory, his slip-ups, and how the secret intelligence service finally cut him loose, providing him with the cover story of prostate cancer. He returned to California, ostensibly to live out his retirement days on the *Doublecross*, a dodgy old trawler in the Vallejo Municipal Marina. To alleviate boredom, he reinvented himself as a fiery Internet pundit supporting right-wing conspiracies and juicy theories about military corruption. He also began teaching a popular night course at the Vallejo Public Library. His "Spotting Spies: Secrets of Espionage Tradecraft" often had a standing room audience.

That night, though, Carver spent time swilling glasses of Templeton's Rye and searching his boat's beat up two-drawer filing cabinet for a dossier of papers he had hidden away. After two hours, he matched spec line drawings from a thirty-year-old top-secret project against a grainy news photo on a website of the *San Francisco Chronicle*.

It was ten p.m. on the West Coast and one a.m. in Virginia but it didn't matter. He punched in the number.

"Uh." The voice had been awakened from a deep sleep. "Who the hell?"

"It's Carver."

"Omigod, Carver. We haven't talked in years. Do you know what time it is?"

"Yeah. But this is important. Have you been following that story about the Coast Guard dredging up an old torpedo hooked to that drug mini-sub?"

"I saw it on the late news. You know, I shouldn't be talking to you. In D.C, you are still poison. The snoops still might have ears on this line."

"Just listen, for a second. You're my brother. George, you're the only person I can call."

"No. This could mean my job."

"It won't. Say I blindsided you. But this is immense. And don't share it with anyone. Not my ex. Not anyone from the agency. What's hanging off the end of the line in Vallejo looks very much like an old SUB-ROC, the nuke-tipped torpedoes from the cold war. With a different warhead collar. I think our muddy fish is a SUBROC that the rogue group at Mare Island might have put together years ago."

"You mean the Trap Door group?" he asked.

"No, Trap Door was a diversion. We called this underground group Mollusk."

There was a long silence. "Carver, are we on a secure line?" he asked.

"No."

"Then hang up and I'll be back on the encrypted phone."

Carver waited. The call came right away. "I'm a bit more awake now and I am understanding what you are saying. You're saying it looks like a SUB-ROC."

"Yeah, but without the five-kiloton warhead."

"I thought the Navy decommissioned all of those," George said.

"We did. I helped with every one of the two hundred and eighty seven SUBROCS. We thought that was the end of it. But there were rumors about a new SUBROC somewhere on the base."

"I heard that chatter. And I heard the Navy thought the group was run by someone they called Tom."

"Yeah. The Navy couldn't find who was doing it. Tom, well, that's what we called him. Major Tom, like the astronaut in the David Bowie song. The Ground Control to Major Tom, who goes on a walk outside the capsule and sees a beautiful world. Anyhow, we assumed that this dissident scientist we called Major Tom was a pacifist. We tried to discredit him, planting rumors that Tom was a user, and hooked on drugs. But in reality, he and his gang had been swiping missile parts and building their own version of a SUBROC. Don't know how they did it, or moved it around. An operational SUBROC loaded with fuel and a warhead weighs around two tons."

"Carver. Any idea where your so-called Major Tom might be?"

"Our one real suspect went to ground in Mexico. In Baja. But our agents never made an arrest."

"So, assume they cooked the books to get themselves SUBROC parts, started modifying them and then, for whatever reason, got cold feet. Maybe they sniffed the Navy was onto them and had to cover their tracks. Let's suppose that they deep-sixed the missile body and final stage solid fuel rocket in the Vallejo channel. We are still missing the warhead. It could be anywhere."

"True. But it might still be valuable. We had heard they made a breakthrough that is a mystery to this day."

"So, do we think any foreign players will come after it?"

"I'd discount the jihadists. Or the Russians or Chinese. Maybe black market freelance arms dealers? And, there are other worries," Carver said.

"Such as?"

"Our own side. Navy lifers with a stick up their butts who covertly might have bought into this or something like it and don't want it to become public. They still have power and might hire a ghost agent to come looking for the nose cone and its workings. That's why I need your help. Someone with cred. See if the mystery dangler stirred any chatter at the Pentagon."

"I'll think about it," he said. "I still don't trust you. And your time on this call is up. But before I hang up, what's your cover story?"

"We're helping the Coast Guard. They have the dangler in the Vallejo yard. Everyone here is retired military and is convinced they know everything about submarines and torpedoes. So, we let it ride that it is a real SUBROC."

"And collateral damage? What about the woman photog who took the news closeups of this SUBROC? Can you find her? I'll bet other agents can find her."

"Well, Maggie, that's her name, is actually my neighbor at the marina. She's smart but innocent. I plan to put the fear of God in her by getting her to work a freelance situation in San Francisco with very dumb but fierce French arms agents. Once she gets exposed to the danger, I'll suggest she take herself out of circulation."

"I won't ask about that."

"No. But I think she'll find out these people don't mess around."

"Okay, but if that doesn't work?"

"Look. Then I'll take care of it," Carver said.

"Carver, you can't let your libido intervene in this. It's much too important."

"Thanks, Brother. Her safety is very important to me. For reasons I'll never reveal. Sorry I didn't ask about Sophie and the kids. Maybe another time. Goodbye."

Carver lay down on his bunk on the *Doublecross* and tried to sleep.

9

Maggie's Gig in the City

I hate Carver. God I hate Carver.

Maggie hadn't knelt this long since she did penance for confessing to dirty thoughts while a Catholic schoolgirl. But that was decades ago. Now she had been down on her knees for twenty minutes on a cold cement San Francisco sidewalk next to a postal storage box that reeked like a campground outhouse.

When I get back to Vallejo, I'm going to kill him for getting me this job.

Her forty-five-year-old body was rebelling. Every muscle still ached from the mid-channel battle saving the Mermaid Queen. Add that to the damage from years of chasing stress-filled news stories. Venturing into sketchy situations. Still, she stayed hunkered down, her Nikon with its telephoto lens resting beside her. These corporate jobs had become her major income. They now paid the bills.

Maggie was pissed. Derrick, the PR director who had hired her over the phone, was a snake. From his droll businesslike phone voice, she expected to meet a corporate type who wouldn't interfere while she shot routine executive portraits.

Nope. Derrick turned out to be a gaunt, nervous little man prone to over-managing the shoot. He demanded Maggie hide behind the mailbox until she could leap out and photo ambush two bigwigs from his company, the Magic Grout firm of Akron, Ohio. He claimed this paparazzi approach would shock the execs into authentic expressions.

Doubtful, thought Maggie. *Waylaying subjects is going to be counterproductive.*

Worse yet, Derrick's unceasing yammer bugged her. It got personal. "Heard good things about your work. I saw your latest photo show on Facebook. Spooky buildings on an old Navy base. Evocative. You certainly don't look like you sound on the phone. Your on-line pix show you with a pretty good shock of red hair. In person, I'd have to say it's gone to gray. Not the most attractive. I mean, with your round face. Didn't expect you to be so old. I don't mean that disrespectfully. Hope you don't mind me talking about your looks. You know, you are carrying a few extra pounds around the waist and your hoodie doesn't really hide it. Exercise more. You'd be more svelte. Try jogging or yoga. You're in charge. Shouldn't depend on the government to take care of you. It's everyone for herself."

His phone buzzed, and he listened. "My source says the party's on. They'll be out of the hotel soon." He poked her on the shoulder. "This is going to be great. Our CEO, Linda Wang Rodgers, is in a black outfit. She'll be with a shorter guy, our marketing manager, in a slick suit. Make sure he is in the shot. The hotel marquee too."

Maggie checked the settings on the camera one final time. The door of the Hotel Triton was thirty yards away. A balding elegantly dressed man wearing dark aviator glasses frowned when he stepped onto Grant Street and into the chill San Francisco afternoon wind. An Asian woman with pale skin and a body-hugging yoga outfit joined him. He slipped his hand under the back of her shirt. She rested her cheek on his shoulder, nibbled on his ear, affectionately patted his ass and brushed something from his suit coat's shoulder.

"These two are all over each other. Doesn't look like. . ."

Derrick cut Maggie off. "Get ready." He bubbled with excitement.

Muscular plainclothes security types with headsets, goatees, and matching mirrored glasses scurried into positions on either side of the couple. These unsmiling bookends scanned the scene and nodded to each other before all four began walking together, heading south down the wide sidewalk, toward Maggie's mailbox hiding place.

"Now." Derrick began jumping up and down and screaming. "Now. Do the paparazzi thing. Shoot it. Now."

Maggie rose from behind her hideaway, steadied the heavy lens against the metal box and fired off twenty frames in rapid succession. She ducked back down.

The couple continued in apparent bliss. But the matching goatees had spotted the camera. Both turned in Maggie's direction.

Derrick leapt up and snatched the shoulder of her hoodie. "Girl, we better run like hell."

It turned into a frantic flight down a nearby cobblestone alley, her bulky Nikon banging around wildly in her backpack. Derrick pushed Maggie into a gap between two trash dumpsters, sat down beside her and pulled three bulging plastic garbage bags and a discarded display of long-stemmed lilies over the top of them. The aroma from coffee grounds and rotting lunch bags plus Derrick's garlic lunch afterbreath was nauseating.

Both watched the subjects of her shoot hurry by the alley.

His hands were shaking when he pointed to the Nikon. "Great. Gimme the shots."

She brushed a banana peel off her jeans. Heart pounding. Sweat trickling down her ribs inside her shirt. This chase was way outside the comfort zone for an out-of-shape photo junkie. Couldn't really catch her breath. Maybe she did need to take up jogging.

It took forever to reach the camera without dislodging the odious bags that were their camouflage. She extracted the tiny memory card from the slot and handed it over. He responded with a wad of cash.

The crumpled bills went into her pocket. She never understood why corporate types like Derrick, an executive with a budget grand enough to hire a freelancer sight unseen at her day rate of eight hundred dollars, would pay off in dirty, untraceable cash.

Derrick zippered the storage card into his jacket. "Thanks. This will be a perfect action shot for the company quarterly report. It shows our CEO in motion. It shows drive. The background is very San Francisco."

"What's next?"

"Nothing. You're done. You've been paid. Be safe. Go home."

"Derrick. Are. . .?"

He put his palm up to interrupt her. Both heard the shuffling of leather soles on the alley's slick surface. Through an opening behind the garbage bin, Maggie could see the two goateed bruisers. They had shaved heads and wore matching black leather bomber jackets. They were speaking in a foreign language she didn't recognize. It sounded French but wasn't. One pointed down the alley.

Derrick frowned. "Oh shit," he said. "We'll chat later."

The thuggish-looking brutes started toward the dumpsters.

"Gotta go," Derrick said. "Don't let those Frenchy flatfoots get you." And he sprang up from beneath the garbage and the flowers, burst into the lane and sprinted away. He had a twenty-yard head start. Leather Jacket Number One took off chasing the speedier Derrick.

Frenchy flatfoots?

Seemed like a weird end to a corporate shoot.

Maggie stayed scrunched down, her heart cycling and throbbing like a gas powered leaf blower. The first pursuer was already off on the chase. She looked around for a weapon and found a child's toy light saber behind the dumpster. As Leather Jacket Two reached the opening, she burst from the garbage pile, yelled, "May the force be with you," and speared him with the rigid plastic toy, catching him just below the Adam's apple and sending him sprawling backwards onto the cobblestones. She bolted in the other direction, slipping through the glass side entrance into the trendy clothing store *Tres Calamaris.*

Don't let them get you?

Crossing *Tres Calamari's* perfumed sales floor and finding another exit would be the perfect escape. She paused in the intimate sleepwear section and turned back to see the thug zigzagging through the brightly lit aisles, pushing shoppers out of his way. She bounded up a wide staircase to the mezzanine.

Maggie stood out in this upscale store. These clothes were outfits for the corporate crowd. Her everyday jeans and fleece hoodie made it clear that she didn't belong. She ducked into a dressing room stall, set her backpack on the floor, held it tight between her knees and pulled the privacy drape across the opening.

Had he seen her? Maggie sat motionless on the changing bench. Didn't dare breathe. Her reflection in the fitting mirror across the claustrophobic booth showed fear. There was no escape and nothing in the booth but a few clothes hangars. She grabbed one and twisted the wire until two unprotected ends stuck out in the front. If it came to that, she figured she would go for his eyes.

The suspense made her queasy. A thug the size of this goon could grab her, toss her to the ground and stomp on her.

Leather Jacket Two had spotted her on the mezzanine. He darted up the stairs and raced to the dressing rooms where he threw open the first curtain. "You're dead. I've got your ass now," he bellowed.

It wasn't Maggie. Instead, a short, sleek woman was concentrating on the curves of her backside in the mirror, satisfied with the alluring skintight fit of new leggings. When the intruder's face appeared, she wailed a heart-stopping ninja warrior yell perfected in her after-work self-defense class, then launched a powerhouse karate straight ahead jab, thrusting the heel of her hand upwards into his nasal cartilage, cracking the nose bone. She followed that with a lightning kick to his crotch before she banged on an alarm button marked "Security". A guard with a walkie-talkie was already heading across the mezzanine toward the dressing rooms.

Stunned and trying to stop a river of blood from his nose, Leather Jacket backed away from the curtain. He didn't see the chrome railing behind him until he cartwheeled over that barrier, dropping six feet to a first floor display bin of women's workout underwear. He flailed for a moment, wiped away fresh blood on something soft and cottony, and struggled to regain his footing before shoving a startled saleswoman out of his way and fleeing with a sports bra draped over his face.

Maggie hurried to the exit on a different alley and joined up with a clot of strolling office workers. There was no sign of Leather Jacket. Turning to run, she collided with an elderly woman using a walker. A few business cards spilled out of her hoodie pocket onto the sidewalk. She gathered up what she could before jumping aboard a trolley car bound for the waterfront. The next commuter ferry heading back across the bay to Vallejo was leaving in ten minutes.

The boat was crowded but once underway there was little chatter. It was the end of the workday. The passengers spread out across a bank of airline-style seats for the trip.

At last, Maggie relaxed. A much needed moment to exhale. She pulled out the greasy clump of twenties from her front pocket and counted them low in her lap. Eight hundred dollars on the nose. Thank you Derrick. That'll pay a few bills. Overall, today's chaos was off the charts weird. Nothing like any freelance job she ever had. She checked her phone. Only one text message but it had no topic line. She deleted it.

That night San Francisco Bay was rough. Swells were running three-to-four feet and the catamaran bucked and heaved on the hour's crossing north to Vallejo, slamming through the chop while spewing out a rooster tail of ethereal mist in its wake. Every jolt shuddered through Maggie's aching skeleton. A massage would be wonderful.

At the terminal on Vallejo's waterfront, the ferry-boat delayed docking for thirty minutes. Everyone on board could smell the pungent marijuana aroma in the air. Deputy sheriffs stood at the gangplank, handing out flyer alerts warning everyone to go home and to shelter in place. This was the third unplanned release from the tests at the new marijuana processing plant. The mayor and city officials who had green-lighted the operation were in for pushback from the frustrated citizens. There would be a well-publicized effort to get the plant managers to fix the problem before ramping up the operation at the end of October.

Maggie hustled to her car. All seemed safe once she was behind the wheel of her ancient but trusty Subaru with the windows shut tight. Its engine started right up and traffic along Mare Island Way was light. She turned down Harbor Way and parked at the Vallejo Municipal Marina lot, slipped from her car, unlocked the security gate, and rushed down the floating dock until she reached the *Angry Duck*. Once inside, she shut the cabin door tight and threw the camera backpack down onto the Formica settee table.

Gusts of wind were whipping up foam and spray in the channel. The swells topped off at three feet, higher than the freeboard clearance on her cruiser, but the marina's riprap breakwater protected the *Angry Duck*. Still, the rougher than normal tidal rocking was soothing.

Living single on the Duck had its benefits. Tonight, however, she craved for someone who might listen to her tale of this most bizarre day. Not her ex Rusty, the sleazeball. No, she thought of calling Mitch. Decompression was her goal. Still, she couldn't dismiss Derrick's rude comments about her appearance. She had always been a short-legged hippish woman with a tendency toward the husky. Now, at forty-five, it was harder to keep the pounds off. And harder to hide that from colleagues.

Her phone buzzed. On the voicemail, there was one number she didn't recognize. The recorded voice sounded like Jaylyn, babbling about the rights to her story.

Maggie made a note to call the Mermaid Queen in the morning. Only then was she content to let the wind clean up Vallejo's weed-besotted air. She poured herself a fresh Aunt Sally IPA and put on the headphones to play a Tove Lo song. This had been a long day.

10
Maggie Goes Viral

U p at dawn, Maggie hopped across to the back deck of the *Doublecross*, and pounded on Carver's cabin door.

He yelled "All right. All right," as he emerged in a terrycloth robe, thinning hair rumpled and sticking up. His voice was raspy. "Bit early, isn't it?"

"No. It's time for some answers," Maggie said.

"Oh. A woman pissed about the gig in San Francisco yesterday."

"Yeah. You knew all about it, didn't you? I worked with a crazy man, got chased by what could have been French thugs, watched a tiny woman warrior decimate a muscle-bound bodyguard, and escaped with a bunch of greasy bills," Maggie said.

"Well, at least you did something famous. Internet famous. You became an instant meme." He held up the printout of a right-wing website with the headline "Scumbag International Arms Dealer and Administration Toady in SF Love Tryst"

Maggie stared at the photograph. "What the hell. That's mine. I took it yesterday."

The attribution was there—photo by Maggie

Trout—and the caption under the picture described the current administration's White House sub secretary to the National Security Agency, Crystal Wang, leaving San Francisco's Hotel Triton following a noisy—according to the hotel's maids—afternoon of undercover horseplay with a well-known French arms dealer René Villancourt. The text speculated today's ambush picture was the kiss of death for Wang's tenure on the President's advisory staff.

"And I've got to tell you Maggie, as soon as I reposted that picture out into the social media world, boy did it go viral. You are now a right wing heroine."

Maggie seethed. "Carver, you son of a bitch. You've got a real dark side and I don't like it. One second it's friendly and the next, you set me up. You're an asshole."

"The answer, my dear, is you shouldn't ever think I am friendly. And yes, Derrick and I used you to expose that bleeding heart liberal security wonk that can't manage her urges. And with that picture you took, Miss Liberal, you are on our side. The righteous patriots of America."

"Oh, you mean the righteous white supremacists. I was very close to getting my ass kicked. You knew the Magic Grout Company shoot was bogus."

"Of course I did. But joining the little scenario outside the hotel will toughen you up for something that's coming in the future," Carver said. "Yesterday's adventure must sharpen your bullshit detector. And, besides, you needed the dough."

"So now I live in fear that your fascist goons might come after me? Especially the one who got kicked in the nuts and had his nose smashed. We've got enough trouble at the marina with simple, stupid burglars."

"They aren't my goons. They're working with arms dealers in Marseille and possibly D.C. I can handle them. However, when you took those pix of the mystery dangler, and they went viral with your byline, you put yourself in their gun sights."

"Carver. You are such a snake. I can't believe you did this to me."

"You'd be wise to disappear for a while."

"I don't back down. But I need you to fix this mess somehow," Maggie said.

"I can partly do that. I know a few Barcelona contacts. Of course, for a price."

"Excuse me."

"You took the job. I know you got paid eight hundred. It'll cost you four hundred to have me put out the fire," Carver said.

"You're charging me?"

"Nothing's free, neighbor. I live on a fixed income. And these thugs are not as stupid as the ones we see in the movies. They strike silently, like when you are snuggled in dreamland in your little cruiser's bunk. Still, I think I can defuse this danger. I am proposing a trade."

"Why should I trade anything with a shithead like you?"

"To save yourself from getting whacked. Here's the deal. You give me hi-res prints of the device they raised and I will take care of things for free."

"Really," Maggie said.

"That's the deal. Get me the prints and the danger disappears."

"Okay, you're on. I'll get you those when I get back from the Delta. By the way, I was told that it was a SUBROC that they pulled up."

"Seemed like that."

"But my Navy submariner guy seemed pretty sure of that," Maggie said.

"That's solid inside information No need for you to Google this further."

Maggie was anxious. In one day, she had become entangled in a shifty business that she didn't ever want. Dangerous news assignments had been one thing but this was totally out of her control.

As she returned to her cabin on the *Angry Duck*, Jaylyn was sitting at the table, playing with the Ruger revolver and an open box of .44 ammo.

"Jesus, Jaylyn. You're back. And what are you doing with my gun?"

"I dropped over for another talk. Saw you were out on your neighbor's deck."

Maggie picked up the Ruger. "Don't fool around. It's dangerous. No safety."

"I loved to shoot. My father used to have a .22 target pistol."

Maggie checked to see if it was loaded. The cylinder was empty. She turned to Jaylyn. "Hey, do me a favor. I left my bag on the back deck. Can you get it for me?"

"Sure, no problem." She slid out and went out to the back deck.

When Jaylyn was outside, Maggie took the Ruger to the front vee-bunk and hid it inside a cavity in the false woodwork. She was back at the table when Jaylyn stepped back with her camera bag.

"So, what's up?"

"I need more advice," Jaylyn said. "I have to meet a very conniving person later today."

"Who is?"

"The mayor."

"Want me to come along for support?"

"Yeah, I'd like that."

"Good. Then later this afternoon, I'm going to take the *Angry Duck* up to a pretty funky little Delta out-post. Would you want to go?"

"Sure. Might be relaxing. As long as the place isn't full of rednecks. They don't like uppity young, black women."

"The people at Serenity are in hiding themselves. And I think they don't really like anyone, white, brown, or black."

"Okay, I'll go with you."

"Good. After we chat with the mayor, you can race home, pack a bag and be back here at two. We'll set out for the Delta on the rising tide.

11

Command Presence

"**O**migod, it stinks in here." The Mayor threw open a window and began waving a file folder to clear the air. The "Don't Smoke My Vallejo" activists had occupied her office and had burned a marijuana stash in the mayoral wastebasket. They also taped news headlines about foul air alerts to the walls and smoked from a stoner's bong atop the mayor's desk while staging a photo op for the *Times-Herald*.

The sheriff's deputies cleared them out minutes earlier.

Hope had finished tidying up when there was a soft knock at the side door. It was eleven a.m. The Commander stood there in his Coast Guard dress blue uniform. "Wow, smells like the BigWeed plant," he said. "I love the official bong out in the open."

"The damn pot plant protestors left it behind." She put it in a closet. "They had a much better time at my desk than I usually have. How are you doing this morning? Please grab a seat."

The Commander ran his fingers along the edge of the polished walnut desk. "You know, this baby is the size of an aircraft carrier. I'm impressed. It has power desk written all over it. I love it."

"It was my father's. The admiral. He passed on but willed this to me. It so much says command presence," the Mayor said. "And it reminds me of him."

"Oh, and I was impressed how you handled those news parasites at the sub-raising press conference. Where did you come up with that 'we have the right to charge access fees bit?'"

"Cities have done it for years. Vallejo made twelve thousand bucks selling access that day. And more licensing the pool video. Every little bit helps."

"I know, but you really put those simpering news jackals in their places."

"Thank you. But you know, I don't hate reporters. We just need the money."

The Commander had run out of small talk and wasn't sure where this meeting was headed. He had called the Mayor's number on the card she slipped into his pocket, and received this invitation. Now he was sitting next to Chipper's dog bed while the dog energetically licked its belly. "Your pooch makes quite a racket."

"Yes, I really wish he wouldn't do all that personal hygiene in public. But I put up with it because he gives me so much love. For the moment, he's my family." Hope had a twinkle in her eye. "Commander, I'm sorry about the clandestine nature of our meeting. I don't need anyone to know I invited you here. That's why I snuck you in."

"Well, if you need a progress report on the…"

"No. Nothing like that. I just wanted to bounce two things off you. We're restaging our yacht parade in a month. Calling it the Re-Sail Festival. Can we count on having a Coast Guard boat to lead it?"

"I'll guarantee it this time," the Commander promised. "You'll love it."

"Also, we've sewn up the film rights to El Gordo's explosion and Jaylyn's flight. What gives with the Coast Guard's review process for feature film scripts?"

"We have an office for those requests. Glorify our role and don't make us look clownish and you'll get the Guard's cooperation."

"Good. I've got one other question." She was smirking. "We are in tune on a lot of levels, so I have to ask—Are you married?"

A sucker punch. The Commander's brain stalled. "Well, that's pretty direct. Currently. You mean currently? Ongoing? No. That ended a few years ago."

"So, I'll be bold. I usually go to karaoke night at Padre Jaime's on Thursday nights?" the Mayor added. "Did you ever think of singing in a bar?"

"You mean the joint by the freeway? Not usually my thing. But I'm free Thursdays. I could give it a try."

"How about nine? You can catch my version of *Unchained Melody*."

"Do I have to sing too?" the Commander asked.

"We'll see. I'll bet you belt it out Semper Paratus in the shower."

"The Coast Guard song. If I could remember the

words? I can do a little Johnny Cash, Willie or maybe some Merle. No, I'm in the country western bucket. And about the shower business, I hope you won't try to visualize that."

The Mayor smiled, stood and looked at her watch. "Oops. Got another appointment." They shook hands and she escorted him to the door. "Aye aye, Commander. Now you'd better go down these back stairs and out the exit that opens to the parking lot. Looking forward to Thursday night."

"Me too."

The Mayor was on a roll. The city's legal department had wrapped up all the copyright legalities for the story of Jaylyn's Flight. The tale solidly belonged to Vallejo. And with the Commander's reassurance, the Coast Guard angle looked clear.

Film offers were pouring in. Two producers had inquired this morning about an auction of the movie rights. A Hollywood talent agency called to say other major studios were working on spec scripts of "The Jaylyn Story". Netflix had set up an appointment to talk about it. RideCo International was developing a daredevil carnival ride on Vallejo's waterfront. It would be called "Mermaid's Flight" and would use stage pyrotechnics and compressed air to cannonball paying participants to an altitude of thirty feet before they landed in a heated water tank. They wanted to test it within a week and open in a month. The mayor made a note to add this to the crucial Re-Sail Fest set for November 2nd.

This whole process was so satisfying that the high voltage mayor had the shudders. Her to-do list was long. Call news assignment editors about Re-Sail. Check on the flakey local sculptor who promises he'll have the Jaylyn in Flight statue done by the next festival. Review contracts with the Chinese guaranteeing shoebox models of El Gordo and the lifelike mermaid dolls will be ready in a month. They should sell like hotcakes at Re-Sail. Next, get the local country band, the Lowlife Squats, to finish writing a tearful ballad about Jaylyn. Make a note to review the first draft of the lyrics.

Hope checked her posture in the mirror on the back of the office door. She stood tall—six-foot-two—and loomed over her opponents. This simple fact of nature guaranteed her leverage in the rough infighting of Vallejo's politics. Even without that advantage, her rivals regarded her as a tough adversary, gritty, feisty, with a quick mind and a wonkish love for policy details. She had taken her city from bankruptcy back to the black. They didn't call her the Monetizing Mayor for nothing.

Politics had never been her goal. After a mediocre undergraduate record at an elite Ivy League college, she headed to New York City, hoping for an entree into the television business. The first break came working nights and weekends as a paid production assistant at the Fox 24-hour cable news channel. There she ran errands for the rising personality Hunter Callahan. Eventually, her telegenic blonde hair, high cheekbones, pouty lips and radiant smile attracted the attention of the cable channel's predatory male bosses. She was promoted to associate producer. Then, a very messy affair at work and her aging father's aggressive dementia forced her give up her New York dreams and return to California.

Back in Vallejo, Hope joined the Solano Republican club and volunteered for committees. Busy most nights, she found herself dropping by her apartment only for a change of clothes. At thirty, she became the youngest ever to hold a Vallejo City Council seat. She loved the energy. She felt born to politics. Three years later, the still youthful-looking candidate, popular with the voters, won the mayoralty.

Now, she was thirty-four. There had been little time for romance. A few straight-laced retired Navy officers, cleared through her father, had taken her out. A self-assured narcissistic developer was sweet on her for a year but she turned down his proposal. On the sly, there were brief hookups with yacht club members and karaoke aficionados. She was much too busy with city business and the interminable night meetings to sustain a long-term romance.

But realities arrived with age. Responding to a feature reporter for a local nightlife magazine, she admitted she might soon be on the prowl for a perfect companion to start a family. "Someone," she told the interviewer, "the equal of that handsome red-haired Fox news personality Hunter Callahan." She never missed his network show, the Callahan Cabal, unless city matters got in the way, and then she recorded it.

Sometimes, she watched the rerun two or three times.

Callahan was the ideal hunk for her. He believed in America and its promise. He savaged liberals every night on his highly rated program. He had that command presence, oozing masculinity, and she knew he could be the lover who would be her equal, someone tall with broad shoulders, someone willing to do all the little tasks in sex and life that she had to do right now. Watching his nightly performance, she would fantasize herself in his arms, and he would whisper, "Let's get out of here." or "You know what's next." And she was ready for that. So until the day he called, she had to make do with the local male population.

At noon, Maggie Trout walked into her office, followed by Jaylyn. Maggie shook hands with the Mayor, and then sat in a chair against the back wall. Jaylyn stood by the Mayor's desk. At six-foot one, the African American college student, born and raised in Vallejo, projected an air of confidence. The Mayor noticed she smelled fresh, like citrus, something the Mayor liked in a woman, and had expressive almond-shaped hazel eyes, the very same color as her own. And, despite a patchwork of facial bruises from the mini-sub explosion, the Mayor judged Jaylyn easily more attractive than herself.

Hope pulled out a chair for her. "Welcome, Jaylyn. Or should I say the Mermaid Queen. Hope you are getting over your injuries."

"Somewhat, thank you."

The mayor put her hand on Jaylyn's shoulder and gave it a pat. "You were really out of it in the hospital.

Anything more the city can do for you?"

"No. I'm good."

"Are you sure?"

"Well, I was curious, about, and how often you prayed for me."

"How often I prayed?" Hope asked.

"In the hospital, you said your thoughts and prayers were with me. So, how often did you pray for me? And to whom? I'm just curious."

"That's all private. You wouldn't want to violate my privacy. Just assume you were prayed for and that's why you got better." The Mayor cleared her throat. "But there are more mundane issues we need to discuss. I am guessing you might have remembered our little conversation about the city of Vallejo copyrighting that day's events. I just wanted to make it clear what parts of the story we own and what parts you own."

"I don't understand."

"Since we paid you a salary, as per the contract you signed, we considered your queenly duties at the Waterfest last Saturday as a work-for-hire, entitling you to a paycheck but giving us intellectual ownership of all aspects of the Waterfest event—including the title Mermaid Queen, the title Jaylyn's Flight, and your body image while in costume."

"And this means what?" Jaylyn asked.

"That we own the story of your spectacular flight. If anyone comes to you for an interview about the opportunities we provided for you, or about the story rights to our Waterfest, please direct them to us.

And use you middle name."

"My middle name?"

"Yes, I believe it is Austin," the Mayor said.

"Yes, but I've never used it."

"It's only necessary when talking about last Saturday or if you sign something that has to do with the Waterfest. You wouldn't want to face felony charges of knowingly violating our copyright. That could mean jail."

"Wait a fucking minute," Maggie yelled. She got up from the chair and walked to stand beside Jaylyn. "What's this jail business? What kind of crappy threat is this?"

"Well," the Mayor said, "She's got to consider the alternatives."

Jaylyn spoke bitterly. "So, I lose my name. You make a ton of loot off my disaster and my looks. In other words, you weren't praying for me, you were preying on me."

"That's a rude statement. I was hoping you wouldn't be contentious about this." The Mayor pulled out a three-foot-tall poster with an enormous blow up of Jaylyn's face, her expression of gleeful rapture as she flew through the air. "These will go up on light poles all over the city. I think you'll like how tastefully we will be marketing our crusade to insert Jaylyn's Flight into the folklore of Vallejo."

Jaylyn's eyes narrowed. "Doesn't look tasteful. It's offensive as hell."

Maggie grabbed the poster, crumpled it up, and attempted to cram it into the wastebasket. She knocked the can over and it rolled across the floor.

Hope continued. "We will also have T-shirts that feature your face, and a line of dolls that look like you in flight. You know, with your arms back. And dreamy eyes. Little girls will be delighted. You will contribute to their happiness."

Jaylyn was stunned. "This is… is so outrageous."

"Well, we took care of your hospital bills, so now we need to recover that money we spent while you relaxed in the ER, lolling about, watching soap operas and eating the food we paid for. Selling swag is how we will do it. You don't want Vallejo to suffer because of you."

"Vallejo? What about me? It's my face on these stupid dolls. You've gone way too far. I'll have to consult a lawyer," Jaylyn said.

"I think you should. However, the copyright is something we own. And your face and body shape in the Mermaid Queen outfit is part of the Waterfest contract. So, when you talk to an attorney, you'll find this is all legal and in order."

Maggie was irate. "Or a big scam. Perpetrated by a dumbass politician. You're going to get pushback on this one, Madame Mayor. You've gone too far."

The Mayor shrugged. "Well, thank you both for coming. And I am certain you will check out the details." Hope circled the desk and sat on the corner by Jaylyn's chair. She was surprised at the sexual attraction she felt for this brainy young university student. "I know this all seems a bit unfair, so I'd like to make it up to you and discuss it further. You and

I are blessed with special stature, we really see eye-to-eye. Maybe I could take you out to a local restaurant for dinner."

"No."

The Mayor handed Jaylyn her official business card. On the back she scribbled the word "Hope" along with a small hand-drawn heart and a phone number. "If you need to carry this conversation further, that's my personal cell."

The next step was to brush back a lock of Jaylyn's hair. Her boss at the cable network always did this to young female interns. But the Mermaid Queen abruptly stood up. "No, Sorry. I've got a boat to catch. I've got to leave."

"Okay, but think about my offer."

Jaylyn stared at the Mayor. "Not a chance, you old bag. I'll see you and that incompetent Wellborn in hell first. And, you'll hear from my attorney." The she turned. "Let's go, Maggie."

Jaylyn dropped the card into a wastebasket beside the desk, and slammed the door as she left. Maggie followed.

The Mayor retrieved the card, and lingered at the window, pulling aside the curtains to watch Jaylyn's strong and supple body stride across the city parking lot.

Hope Stinger knew this woman might get the best of her at some point. She just didn't know when.

12
Serenity Point Landing

Vallejo sits southwest of the vast and chaotic Sacramento River Delta, a thousand-square-mile maze of rivers, sloughs, estuaries, waterways, and farming islands guarded by high levees. This landscape is home to hundreds of gunk-hole harbors, modern commercial marinas, dodgy trailer parks and hidden outposts, where a suspicious population lives along the water's edge, staying under the radar.

Serenity Point is a Delta backwater landing two hours by boat east of Vallejo. Its glory days as an anchorage ended years ago with the natural silting of its channel. Faded, listing cruisers and half-sunk liveaboard sloops now bob in a narrow waterway amid rotten docks surrounded by water hyacinths. Half its thirty slips are useless. Two pontoon houseboats anchored next to the pot-holed boat launch ramp spend half their time bottomed on the mud. A few residents squat in decaying fiberglass cruisers marooned on trailers in the parking lot. Goats roam freely in a junkyard of old outboard runabouts, rusty vans, and wrecked cars.

In the 1970s, two women workers from Mare Island Shipyard, Erika Pazty and Teresa Almeda, pooled their money and bought these three acres of remote levee shoreline. They wanted to start a Buddhist retreat, a getaway haven for study and exercise. Over time, they trucked in lumber and built a modest wooden structure with a meeting room, bare bones kitchen, a dormitory bedroom and a simple bathroom. They decided their refuge should be named Serenity Point.

All went well until the Navy pulled out of the Mare Island Shipyard in 1996. After that, many who enjoyed the retreat at Serenity left town and the owners had to sell. A land developer bought it, built a pier for a landing, brought in the floating docks for a marina, and registered the name Serenity Point. But that scheme failed, and Erika Pazty purchased it back for a song in a bank auction.

Over time, a new live-aboard community migrated to the spot for its isolation. They converted the abandoned Buddhist retreat into a meeting spot, adding an outside deck with two tables made from industrial wire spools. Despite not having food for sale, they called it the Shipwreck Cafe at Serenity Point Landing.

Maggie took great care maneuvering the Duck through the sloughs and estuaries en route to Serenity. Even at high tide, the water lapping against the shorelines is only knee deep and the navigable channels are beset with intrusive vines and debris. Any boat a few yards off the centerline is a candidate for grounding and a tow. As she approached, she phoned her half-sister Promise.

Promise stood by while Maggie edged into a transient slip. She caught the line and knotted it on a cleat. Maggie leaped ashore, followed by her passenger. "Watch out," Promise cautioned. The floating dock had rotted in places and boaters had to step gingerly to avoid falling through the wood.

"Promise, this is Jaylyn. She was the one who was blown up at the Waterfest. I told her this was a good place to get herself back together."

Promise eyed Jaylyn. The women shook hands. "Well, here we have the quietude. And I can find you a bunk somewhere afloat. Dennis is off to Alaska for the salmon season, so I'm watching his boat. His cabin is a mess but you can use its bunk. If you stay for long, know that our philosophy here is self-reliance, so I may ask you to work in the vegetable garden at times. And, possibly, pay rent."

"Fine by me. As long as I don't get hassled by backwoods rednecks around here," Jaylyn said.

"Can't promise. But most everyone here is a little bit hermit, so nobody should bother you.

"Who runs this place?" Jaylyn asked.

"I do. I am the owner. Come on, I'll show you to my boat," Promise said.

They walked to a half-gutted seventy-year-old Chris Craft cruiser, the *Henry David*. "I named it after Thoreau. I loved *Walden*. His message of self-reliance is now my mantra. We call our life here in Serenity—Waldonian."

Jaylyn jumped aboard. Half the old boat was taped off behind plastic sheeting. Promise was matter of fact about it. "Yeah, this baby burned two years ago when I dropped a cigarette during a varnishing operation. The fire got pretty intense. It was my fault. I gave up smoking after that."

"So you only live on half of it?"

"Yeah, the whole forward dinette and cabin are gone. The engine compartment and wiring harness burned. It'll never go to sea again, but I can still live in the aft stateroom."

"How long have you been in Serenity?" Jaylyn asked.

"On and off, since I was a little kid. At one point, I was working as an artist in San Francisco and was happy until my mother announced she needed a life-changing journey of discovery. That's her bullshit cover story to explain that she was running from the feds. Anyhow, she deeded this land to me and I came back to try and make a go of it. There is steady dough from rentals, a bit more from growing organic veggies in riverbank plots for local farmers' markets, and I pick up a little by hawking hand-painted refrigerator magnets to tourists at the nearby upscale Bethel Island Marina."

Promise, Maggie, and Jaylyn were sitting down to coffee when a man stumbled out from behind the clear plastic sheeting. Maggie was taken by his deep brown skin and patchwork of colorful body tattoos across his chest, arms and neck. He was wearing shorts and was buttoning a rumpled shirt.

Promise squirmed a bit. "This is a friend of mine. Meet my half-sister Maggie and her friend Jaylyn."

"Hey, friend," Maggie said, extending her hand. "Nice tats."

The man ignored her, mumbled and looked uncomfortable. He stretched, and then touched Promise on the forehead before stepping outside and jumping to the dock.

Both women grinned at Promise. She squirmed. "All right, you guys, don't give me a hard time. Okay."

There was silence. Promise smiled. "Hey. It's a fling. Nothing long-term. Just for the moment. He's a found-object artist who lives in Manhattan Beach, in Los Angeles. He's leaving today. I probably won't see him again."

Promise turned to Maggie. "So, on the same subject, whatever happened to your cute guy named Mitch. Did you two have a blowup?"

Maggie shrugged. "We never really had a together. Now we are not talking."

"But you kind of liked him? Told me he was worth a trial run."

"I did. But we kept misfiring. And he humiliated me. So, now, it's nowhere."

Everyone heard new footsteps along the boat's railing. The face of a heavy-set middle-aged woman with sparkling eyes appeared at the cabin door.

"Hello. Hello. Good morning. I'm Krista."

There was an awkward silence. Finally, Maggie stood up, stuck her hand out. "Hi Krista. Anything we can do for you?"

"I am the mother hen of a student group from Iceland working on Bethel Island this summer. I've come to meet you."

Maggie laughed. "Krista, come on in. Don't be bashful. This is Promise. And over there is Jaylyn. You're a ways from Bethel Island?"

"Well, we are from the National Church of Iceland and are in the Delta on a United Nations High Commission on Squalor project to rejuvenate the deplorable conditions affecting communities throughout the world. We're focusing on the Delta but our original destination at Bethel Island wasn't deplorable enough. It has too many upscale marinas and trailer parks. So, now we are branching out, looking around for squalor and I wanted to see if Serenity Point qualifies. My first impression is that this is a prime example of shabby poverty, with questionable drinking water and near non-existent sanitary facilities. The U.N. wants to involve the local residents in depressed areas like Serenity to build new sanitations," Krista said.

"Sanitations?" Maggie asked.

"Bathrooms," Krista answered.

"New bathrooms would be cool," Promise said. "The one we have at the Shipwreck here in Serenity is stinky and slimy with mold and insects."

"Promise, you are right. Old ones breed disease and depression. The Squalor Project believes that where you sit determines your outlook on life, and what you smell will stop you from contributing to the development of your region."

Promise seemed excited. "So do we get the new showers too?"

"Well, right now, we are just looking around. We have many other communities to investigate."

Maggie spoke next. "Krista. You seem a bit old for a student?"

"I'm forty-five. Yes, old enough to be a mom to the others, but when I heard of this project, I enrolled at the University to get a trip to this part of California."

"Then you are exactly the same age as myself and Promise here," Maggie said. "I'm curious why you are doing this. Do you get paid?"

"Well, yes, a token salary. It's not much. But we all have other reasons for coming here. Mine are very personal and too complicated to explain."

"So, Krista, I suggest we take all your salaries and add it to the money the U.N. is spending on your living quarters and food and just hire a contractor to build us new bathrooms."

"No, you are ahead of yourself. We haven't even chosen out target spots yet."

Maggie looked over at Promise, rolled her eyes and smirked. She pointed to the galley. "So, Krista, it's nice to meet you. We were just about to have a cold refreshment. Want a margarita?" she asked.

"Isn't it a bit early for that?"

"So, what time is it in Reykjavik?"

"It's seven hours ahead."

"So, it's about midnight there?"

Krista smiled. "I see what you are saying. A margarita would be wonderful. Then I'll take you on a tour of our motorhome."

13

Mitch Passes on the News

For years, Maggie had loved spending Delta mornings relaxing on the aft deck of the *Angry Duck*, sipping a peaceful cup of coffee with her ex husband Rusty. They would sit for hours in the dew-damp canvas chairs, watching flights of stately Canadian Geese wheel in for a landing. The earthy swamp smell filled the air. But now her cheating ex was wrapped in the arms and perfumes of his teenage aromatherapist and Maggie was left sitting alone on this deck. Oddly, she found the tranquility of the place even more captivating.

Except when her cellphone interrupted.

"Yo."

"Maggie. Just wanted to update you on the action back at the Marina."

"Mitch. Please don't tell me there have been more burglaries?"

"No. No, not that. No, this is about Captain Blowhard."

"What happened? Is Carver okay?" Maggie asked.

"Don't know. Last night, he didn't show for his night class in spy tradecraft at the library. I came back to the marina and knocked at his boat's door. Nothing. Then I checked our surveillance video and spotted unidentified characters hanging around D dock. And now, Carver is missing from his boat."

"Did those guys have shaved heads and leather jackets?"

"Too dark on the video to see," Mitch said. "Not sure if I should worry. It's only been twelve hours, but he's not on the *Doublecross* or at a local bar or the *Can* for breakfast. I checked this morning's surveillance video. Didn't see him."

"Did you call the cops?" Maggie asked.

"I did. They came and looked around but said it was too soon to do anything. They said they would follow up on those intruders."

"Well, maybe Carver's off on a right-wing day trip somewhere. Keep me posted if and when he turns up."

"Will do. And if you are coming back this way and need a temporary slip, I still have a few on B dock. I see you are up in Serenity Point."

"You see I'm where?"

"Up at Serenity Point. I've hooked one of my startup's Findola tab GPS targets onto every Marina boat. We're beta testing our laser-targeted micro-fob that sticks to the hull and helps first responders to find a boat in trouble. I think we've solved most of the software bugs and it'll be ready for release soon. It leaves a GPS trace, so a site manager can find a present position like yours up in Serenity."

"That's a freaking invasion of privacy."

"No, the beta test is a service of our Marina. In three months, we hope to begin selling it to harbormasters everywhere," Mitch said.

"All right. Tomorrow, I'll need that temporary on B dock. Any news on that thing they dredged up?" Maggie asked.

"You mean El Gordo's torpedo? The Coast Guard has it at their yard next to the *Sardine Can*. The latest dope is—no explosives on the dangler. But the warhead is missing and that seems to bother everyone."

"Well, keep me posted on Carver. I'll see you mañana. Bye, Mitch."

Jaylyn emerged from the Duck's cabin barefoot and wearing light tan sweatpants and a taco stand T-shirt with the word "Hot". She stretched. "Well, I slept most of the night. Feels good."

"Yeah, it's peaceful. Nothing moves fast in the Delta."

"You're right. This is calm city." Jaylyn yawned. "Might start to get interesting tomorrow though. The weird Squalor Project wants to have a conversation with us at two o'clock."

"For what?" Maggie asked.

"I guess the toilet business," Jaylyn said."

"Well, if it works out, Promise should like that. After all, her idol Thoreau built his own outhouse at Walden. At least he said he did. But hand building a modern septic system with complex plumbing seems impractical," Maggie said.

"Maggie, where you off to?"

"Gotta take the Duck back to Vallejo."

"Well, I'm thinking of staying here for a few days."

"I think that's a good idea. After you and Promise go to the meeting, keep me posted."

Before noon, Maggie guided the *Angry Duck* into the transient tie-up at the end of the Vallejo marina's B dock. Mitch was there and waved her over to a nearby slip. He took the line and tied it off on the cleat.

This hospitality didn't lessen Maggie's anger. "Mitch, thanks for the tie-up but you are a complete sack of shit. You know. Every time I think of that horrific song, or whatever you call it, that you sang at the city council. It was humiliating."

"Just trying to be heartfelt," Mitch said.

"So you made my award all about your stupid song."

"No, if anyone heard the next three verses to the ballad, it was your story."

"No one will," Maggie said.

Mitch tied off her aft line. "OK. So I'm sorry. You can use this slip for now."

"Heard from Carver?" she asked.

"Nothing. Not a peep."

"This worries me."

"Oh, he's tough enough to stay out of trouble. Besides, one of his old spook buddies is in town, and she's looking for you."

"Spook?" Maggie asked.

"Yeah. Don't tell me you didn't guess. Carver was a raging spook in D.C. You can tell that from his library class. But that was back when he was at the top of his form."

"So, who is here?"

"She wouldn't say but she's got enough make up on to cover a lot of wrinkles. She's been hanging in the office, watching your little blue dot sail through the Delta. And here she comes now."

A thin older woman with styled short gray hair, a pale face, and prominent ears was walking along the dock. She wore a professional outfit of black slacks, a black turtleneck sweater and a blue wind-breaker. Even from the distance, Maggie could see she was not smiling.

"Thanks, Mitch. I'll take it from here," Maggie said.

The visitor stuck her hand out. "You must be Maggie. I'm Valerie Beckett. A longtime colleague of Carver's from D.C. I heard from sources that he might be in trouble." There was an awkward pause. "Call me Val."

"Is he still missing?"

"Yes, missing per se. For fifteen hours now. Might just be out of touch. No one is sure." Valerie scanned the dock area. "Can we go inside your boat?"

"Sure," Maggie said.

They sat down at the foldout settee table in the galley. "Do you want coffee?" Maggie asked.

"Only if you've got de-caf. My docs say I have to

drink that stuff. It's usually brown water. But if you have any herbal tea, I'll take some of that."

"I've got rooibos?"

"Sure. That'll do."

Maggie heated up the kettle and popped a cup of coffee in the microwave for herself.

"Maggie, I'm going to tell you a story so you'll have a little background about what's going on."

"Do I have a choice? No offense, Val, but I'm not eager to get involved."

"Yes, I understand. But Carver worried you had no choice."

"Because I took pictures of the sea bottom weapon?"

"Exactly. And that's why Carver thought he could scare you by setting you up on that bizarre photo shoot with the French agents."

"You know about that? How do you know about that? That was no fun. So you'll understand why I'm not ready for any cooperation with you."

"Ah, but taking those up close shots sealed your fate. Your pictures could be very valuable for certain actors in the international arms trade. The most crucial action for you now—stay vigilant. And trust very few."

"This whole situation is a bunch of shit." Maggie said.

"Most of our work is. Here's the backstory. In the 80s and 90s, during the Cold War global superpower standoff, dangerous missiles and hot lines were what kept the planet from blowing itself to shreds in a thermonuclear cataclysm. All the sides built arsenals, despite stand down treaties. Mare Island was in the middle of it. There were conspiracy theories here about leaks and embedded agents. Speculation surfaced about a secret organization called Trap Door. But Trap Door was a dirty tricks rumor put out by the Navy. It worked as a diversion. In 1996, when the military walked away, the Navy had never found any solid evidence that a group was working out of the box. Just rumors. Your dockside neighbor, Carver Pardon, was big in that search. They constantly screened and spied on the workforce for information leakers and foreign agents."

"Spied?" Maggie said.

"Oh yeah. They had listening devices everywhere. Bars. Dance halls. The officer's club. Even the old submariner's bar, the Horse and Cow. They were intensely focused on what they called the Mollusk project, a rebellious clique working on clandestine weapons made of simple materials. This group was proficient at staying underground," Valerie said.

"Please don't tell me this stuff. Like I said, I really don't care for your games. I have a mild interest in finding Carver, but I'll skip your scummy secret world."

"Well, none of it except the name Mollusk is secret now. You can find the rest on Wikipedia. Apparently, these dissidents were developing non-nuclear ersatz warheads for weapons. Bone up on this. Events could get very hairy soon."

"So, what does this Mollusk group have to do with me?"

"The torpedo they pulled up from the mini-sub might have been theirs."

"And are they behind Carver's disappearance?"

"Who knows? We don't know who they were or where they are now. And Carver is an enigma. He may be behind his own disappearance. In his prime, his mind was sharp. The equal of anybody in the espionage business. But lately, he's been a bit dotty. Forgetful. Right now, we don't trust Carver. Be suspicious of anything he does. And be suspicious if anyone shows up unannounced snooping around. That's all I can tell you."

Maggie refilled her coffee cup. Valerie still had plenty of tea. "Okay, tell me this. A woman appeared yesterday at my sister's landing in the Delta. Said she was working with the United Nations and they were doing a project in California to alleviate poverty. Should I be suspicious?"

"I would. The community development angle is not an unusual cover story in our world. You say it's the U.N. I'll check it out for you," Valerie wrote in a small notebook.

Maggie took another sip. "Do you think Carver is all right?"

"Like I said. That's a million-dollar question. But until we know more, we should construct a plan to search for him. Carver said that you are familiar with the deserted factory buildings and warehouses on the old Mare Island property. That you know your way around MINSY."

"I do. I've been prowling MINSY for the past four years. I know most of the building numbers, and which ones are occupied with startup companies or artists' collectives. There are plenty of empty ones."

"Good. Let's make a map of abandoned buildings you think might be important. There are also rumors of a hidden lab we need to find. I'm afraid we'll have to do this on the sly. We're looking for a place they might keep someone, somewhere in an old workshop or storage room."

"Okay, I'll get a map together."

"How's your schedule? Doing any free lance shooting this week?" Valerie asked.

"I have one gig. Tomorrow is going to be Vallejo's bizarre moment in history. Our crazy mayor has contracted with an amusement park company and they are going to test the prototype of a goofy ride called Mermaid's Flight. Blasting someone into the channel. I really should shoot that."

"Good. After that, we'll meet up about looking."

"We? I haven't said yes yet."

"Sorry. But once you snapped that photo of the SUBROC, you signed on for the duration. There's no backing out now."

14

Mermaid's Flight is Readied

For days, Vallejoans enjoyed a brief respite from the dangling torpedo media swarms. Shoreline streets and the nearby downtown returned to an everyday calcified calm. But a new flashpoint was begging for another invasion by the media. Vallejo's publicity savvy mayor had done her best to re-wiggle the city's events into the nation's news limelight.

This time, the omen for it all was a pair of enormous Fox News semi-trucks that rumbled in and parked along the shoreline. Crews began setting microwave dishes, laying long broadcast cables and building a temporary news anchor desk. Then pushy reporting teams began roaming the town, approaching any public clot of more than two citizens to get reaction to what was coming next.

The curiosity today was the real world testing for RideCo's prototype of the Mermaid's Flight carnival ride. A crowd of bystanders had gathered around the company workers readying the launch machinery at shoreline park. They yelled questions at the RideCo workers who were making adjustments to the compressed air cannon—it would fire a ticket holder from the shoreline and send that paying client one hundred yards downrange to a landing in a warm freshwater pool.

"Someone's really going to get into that?"

"That's the craziest fucking deathtrap I've ever seen."

Finally, a hardhat-wearing company rep walked over to them.

"You wait. You'll see. This is safer than sitting on a portable toilet."

The onlookers groaned.

And they were right. The initial firings were disappointing. The first human-sized sandbag, fired out in a cloud of stage smoke, only flew ten feet before somersaulting into the frigid channel water. The next sandbag veered off course and smashed through the second floor windows of the Mare Island Brewing Company, interrupting the afternoon drinkers mildly engrossed in the stimulating telecast of a Canadian bull-riding rodeo. Three more sand bags dropped hopelessly short.

The bystanders jeered. News cameras recorded every flop. Engineers worked on the barrel elevation, adjusting it until fifteen straight tests landed in a warm water tank one hundred yards from the cannon. Then they pronounced it ready.

There was polite applause from the growing crowd.

The Mayor had planned today's schedule so the first human test shot would coincide with the East

Coast taping of Hunter Callahan's Fox News show, the Callahan Cabal, originating from New York and broadcast nationally. The show's producers were delighted to air this screwball event, promising a fifteen-minute segment.

Hope had a hidden purpose besides the marketing of the Vallejo Brand. She confided to friends that today might finally be her chance to connect with Hunter Callahan's heart. She spent hours at a local salon where they re-dyed her roots and added red highlights into her blonde coif. A makeup artist worked on her face, outlining her pouty lips and softening the first wrinkles by her eyes. Another gave her hair a stunning blow-dry. Her confidants approved an outdoor casual outfit that complimented her tall, willowy figure. And her Pilates trainer assisted with her personal Zen mantras to supercharge her pheromones, making them so potent they would reach across the airwaves.

After all, she had carried this torch for Hunter since her years as a production assistant at the cable channel.

On the shoreline, the RideCo testing was on standby. The crew was waiting for the first human guinea pig, a Hollywood stuntwoman, to show up. She was late.

The Mayor arrived at the location, toting Chipper in an over-the-shoulder purse. She strode confidently to the improvised Fox News site. Stagehands ushered both to a plywood riser and impromptu anchor desk for her interview on the Callahan Cabal. Seated at the temporary news set and outfitted with an earpiece, the Mayor went through a microphone check.

On the monitor screen placed at her feet, she saw the image of Hunter Callahan with the words "New York". Her pulse raced and her mouth went dry. Within seconds, her face appeared on the other half of the screen, with the word "Valleho". Hope considered whether to make a fuss out of East Coast misspelling but in the end, she let it go. After all, she and Hunter were together at last.

As his program began in New York, Hunter rushed through an arrogant and aggressive leadoff segment, humiliating a California Democratic congresswoman for arguing women's health care was a right. "Owning a gun is a right," Callahan opined, "but health care is a commodity you should buy when you need it."

Before Fox ran a commercial, Hunter teased the Vallejo story. "We'll be visiting a California city that encourages its tourists to fly." After the break, he showed video of the Waterfest mini-sub debacle, and then watched as Hope's picture came up again to share the screen with his. "Mayor Hope Stinger is with us. And let me say, Hope, that it is good to see you again. Hope was once part of our newsroom Fox family here in New York. Now she's the top executive of a bustling California town. Mayor Stinger, we've seen the background on the amusement ride your city is developing. Can you tell me what the viewer can expect?"

"Well, Mr. Callahan, it's our first day for testing. And the ride is all American. Vallejo demanded that. Even the sandbags are filled with American sand. We're using American sound design to replicate the explosive noise from the original sub explosion and American theatrical stage smoke for the visual. Once Mermaid's Flight is operational, visiting tourists and others will get a chance to experience what our native daughter Jaylyn Chadwick felt when she got the ride of her life during our Waterfest Weekend last month. We call the brave adventurers who dare to fly Jaylyn-a-Nauts."

"And so, is everything ready for today's test?"

"That's an a-okay, Mr. Callahan. Aye aye it is."

"Before you launch, I have to clear up one exotic detail. Stories in the tabloid press and blogosphere have claimed that this ride may produce unusual stimulation, something that might result in an afterglow. Is it true?" Callahan asked.

The Mayor smiled slightly "You mean sensational accounts suggesting powerful happy endings."

"Yes. That's a good way to put it. At least as much as we can do on a family program."

Hope had a twinkle in her eye. "Sorry, I can't confirm or deny, Mr. Callahan."

"Well then, are you ready to push the button that will launch the first test, as you call them, of your Jaylyn-a-Naut?"

"I am, Mr. Callahan."

An aide rushed up and whispered in her ear. The

mayor grimaced. "Mr. Callahan, and all of America, we have a so wee delay. It seems our stunt woman is so stuck in traffic."

"That's too bad, Mayor. I sure wanted to see this work. Is there anyone else out there who might fill in?"

"Not standing by."

"We are on a tight deadline. Maybe you could sit in for the first ride?" Callahan suggested.

"Mr. Callahan, I'm not sure I am dressed for that."

"Come on Hope. You were a standout part of our news team years ago. Where's that spontaneity? That drive I remember and cherish."

"I'm not certain I should do this," the Mayor said.

"Hope. I can see in your eyes you have a desire to make Vallejo great again. Go ahead. Take a chance. I would. And I will respect you when you do."

Hope thought it over for ten seconds.

"Okay," she said. "This one is for you." The Mayor unhooked her microphone and stepped off the riser. She grabbed a reluctant Chipper and walked to the air cannon. Within seconds, workers had tucked her blond tresses into a crash helmet, and had strapped the automatic parachute harness over her pristine LL Bean silk camping blouse. Dressed for flight, she snuggled into the cannon's barrel, cradling Chipper in her left arm. He wore a leather flying helmet and goggles.

On the set, Hunter Callahan's demeanor was changing. It appears Hope's Cupid-like hyper-pheromones

had indeed defied the laws of physics and had tran-
sited the airwaves. An arrow of desire befuddled
Hunter. He gazed at the monitor, with a gooney grin
on his face. His voice was deep with concern. "Let
me know when you are ready?"

Hope looked mildly apprehensive but gave the
thumbs up. The ride attendants closed the Plexiglas
canopy to the cannon barrel. Callahan began a countdown from New York that was piped over the shoreline public address system.

"Five."

"Four."

"Three."

"Two."

"One."

"Bombs away, I guess."

An explosive concussion rocked the shoreline.
Smoke billowed from the launching cannon. The
cameras recorded the next moments as the
Honorable Hope Stinger's form rose out from the
miasma like a rocketless cosmonaut leaving the
launch pad. Her helmet glinting, she hurtled skyward
with a goofy look on her face, finally spreading her
arms behind her in a cross, her body shuddering while
sailing along a smooth, arcing ballistic track downrange. Chipper flew beside her, his paws spread, his
eyes protected by the goggles, but wearing an inane
smile.

The calculations were perfect. The Mayor and
Chipper splashed down on target in the tank of warm

water. Both popped quickly to the surface and dog-paddled to the tank's rim. Attendants helped remove the parachute. Hope's worry about her revealing clothes was well founded. The wet blouse had become transparent, showing off her assortment of skimpy French underwear.

A Fox stagehand handed her a robe and clipped a microphone on it. She whispered into Hope's ear. "Hunter will be speaking to you. I've never seen him so emotional. You seem to have pierced his deflector shield. Tell him how you feel, Mayor. Speak to him. This is your moment. Be heartfelt."

In the New York studios, Hunter could barely control himself. "Thank heavens you are safe. You were looking mighty happy in flight, my dear."

Hope appeared dizzy. "That was something, Mr. Callahan," she blurted out, almost breathless. "Omigod. Omigod. You know, I'm hungry now. Hungry for food. Our Mermaid Queen was right. This ride stimulates so much rapture. A shudder rose from my ankles. I don't know if I can say this on Fox, but I've just had the most intense happy ending of my entire life."

The crowd applauded.

Chipper was perky. "Woof," he barked, as he humped Hope's leg with enthusiasm.

Hunter grinned. "That Chipper looks happy. Wish I was there with you, rubbing your calf, Hope."

The stagehands looked at each other and rolled their eyes.

"Mr. Callahan, I don't know what to say. You are certainly welcome to visit Northern California and stop in Vallejo when you do. I'd like that."

"Hope, it's true. Give me a few days. I'll be there."

In the darkened New York control room, the show's producer looked over to the director. "I don't like where this is going," she said. "He's way off script."

"I can take you on that ride. Come to the glorious Re-Sail Festival next month," Hope said. "We'll do it as many times as you like."

"That's quite an invitation," Hunter said. His voice had softened to a whisper.

"You'd get to meet Chipper too."

"I'd love to. I'll be there much sooner and bring a handful of doggie treats."

"Don't forget treats for me," the Mayor said.

The producer had covered her face with the script pages. She mimed a mock prayer to the heavens. "Please stop him. He's getting mushy. In ten years, I've never seen him lose his caustic edge. Maybe we insert a commercial and slap him around."

"I'll check the log," said an assistant.

But it was too late. Viewers could see Hunter Callahan squirming. "America, I knew this day would happen. I don't know what's come over me. I've been doing this show for ten years. A certain sameness has set in. I am tired. It's time for new blood. There's always a young gunslinger in the shadows waiting to swap lead with the old man. I defer to that person.

My spirit is demanding a change."

The producer stood up in the darkened control room. "Omigod. Stop him," she shouted. "He's going to quit."

The two-hour program was only thirty minutes old when Hunter Callahan abdicated his anchor chair.

"And now loyal viewers, I say these ten years have been a good run. Take care, everyone." Violating all union rules, Hunter Callahan unclipped his own microphone, set it gently on the anchor desk, stepped off the riser, and headed for his dressing room. "I'm done," he said.

Hunter Callahan's abrupt mid-show walk-off at Fox became a tabloid sensation. Within hours, his multi-million-dollar Manhattan love nest condo was on the market. The next afternoon, after a grueling red-eye transcontinental flight, he was spotted shopping real estate in the Napa Valley.

The *Times-Herald* put out a special edition with the banner headline in three-inch letters reading "Mayor Takes a Leave". The story rambled on about the test firing of the Mermaid's Flight cannon and Hope's newly kindled steamy hookup with a national cable hunk. The city council president and new interim mayor lamented Hope's loss but said "Vallejo will continue to prosper without her."

Although Hope disappeared from Vallejo, she was not far from the hearts of her former townspeople.

That same day, nosy citizens posted Facebook videos showing her browsing at a Pottery Barn discount outlet in Napa, and buying dishes and linens at the Oxbow Public Market. She waved a good-natured greeting. Everyone knew. She was due for a rendezvous with Hunter that night.

Hunter had prepared, renting a luxurious condo on the eighth hole of an exclusive gated community golf course, stocking the place with his trademark inducements of flowers, champagne, music, candles, condoms and a set of backlit Texas longhorns above the headboard. Tonight was to be the magic beginning, an introduction for Hope and her pheromone barrage to the love-making artistry of a man *New York* magazine once rated among the ten sexiest studs in Manhattan. Callahan watchers wondered if he was off the deep end. They knew very well about his disdain for commitment to a long-term relationship. The answers would come tonight.

At precisely six p.m., Hope arrived at the love nest condo, mouth dry, skin showered and fresh, carrying groceries and her suspicious mutt Chipper. She was primed. Before a word was said, Hope and Hunter fell at each other in the doorway, their hands roaming in a frenzy. Savage kisses led Hope to drop the food and the dog to the floor. In a flash, they were unbuttoning each other's clothes, stumbling down the hall, crashing against walls, creating a sweaty erotic tornado as they headed toward the longhorn festooned headboard in the bedroom.

Only one roadblock could derail the brewing love

storm—Chipper. Jilted at the door, not a dog treat in sight, he had to sit and watch a half-naked interloper teevee personality struggle to pull Hope's balky long sleeved jersey over her head.

Until the back zipper caught on her ponytail.

"Eiiiiiii," she screamed. But the frantic Hunter, mistaking this for a libidinous exultation of great joy, pulled harder, finally ripping hair from her scalp while tearing the jersey in half.

"Halt. For godsakes stop," Hope yelled.

Clipper decided to stop this attack on his cherished master. In a defensive rage, Chipper sprang at Hunter with barred teeth, reaching the Fox news anchor's midsection and clamping down on his privates. After a blood-curdling scream and wrestling match, it took a few seconds for the reigning New York stud to get the upper hand, prying apart the terrier's jaws, then smacking Chipper and knocking him silly. Hunter grabbed a pristine Pottery Barn dishtowel to staunch the bleeding before Hope drove him to the nearby Queen of the Valley Hospital, where the doctors treated his wounds with stitches, antibiotics, and snickers. When Hunter was sedated for an overnight stay in the ICU, Hope returned to the condo.

She had feared this moment, always knowing there would be a decision about a canine impediment to her breeding future. Forced to balance loyalty to her spoiled Chipper against the dream of a lifelong relationship, she knew she had to act.

Chipper jumped up onto her bed. "Bad dog. Bad

dog," she admonished. But Chipper did not appear remorseful. He looked like a giddy pet that had just rolled in a dead seagull. That was the deal breaker. Fuming, she picked up the leash. "Dog park. Dog Park," she said rattling the leash clip. Chipper wagged his tail and ran for the front door. In less than five minutes, Hope had stopped at the Vallejo Benicia Animal Shelter and handed over Chipper to the pound attendants. "Find him a home. He's so much a pest," she said. Then she spun and walked out the door without even a look back.

The next morning, Queen of the Valley doctors were quick to advise Hunter Callahan that his injuries would prohibit him from performing certain husbandly bedroom functions, at least for the next six months and maybe forever. The very idea. The prodigious Hunter Callahan, a reigning prince among the top echelon of fornicating bed jockeys in Manhattan, was now on the disabled list and out of action.

Hunter steamed at this news, and soon had his publicist send Hope an email declaring that it was over between them. He hired a private hospital plane to take him back to New York City. Although the flight began after midnight from a remote spot at Napa's airport, Maggie and a herd of jackal-like paparazzi got word and photographed him on a gurney with bulging bandages protecting his masculine tools. New York's Daily News ran the humiliating picture, credited to Maggie Trout, on the front page with the headline, "Fabled Newsie's Left Coast Love Adventure Ends with a Bite."

The big loser here was Chipper. The always self-absorbed terrier had to assume the role of a dog begging for a new home. After all, the kennel could only keep him two weeks and then, well, they needed his enclosure. But in a stroke of luck, a pet adoption Facebook editor featured the former First Dog of Vallejo whimpering in the back of his cage. A banner across the bottom of the video stated his case. "Abandoned".

15

Mitch Gets a Pet

Mitch had never looked after a pet. Not as a child. Not as an adolescent. He did get an ant farm as a birthday present once but traded it at school for baseball cards. However, after seeing Chipper's pleading eyes in a photo on the Next Door Internet web site, then reading the *Times-Herald* front-page tearjerker story of the mayor's former pooch languishing at the pound, he knew he had to move fast. Mitch not only liked the little terrier but also suspected there was a modicum of political strategy in this.

He drove like a madman to the county animal shelter, and burst through the front door, announcing to the receptionist, "What's it take to rescue that dog, Chipper?"

"Well," replied the soft-spoken woman at the front desk, "you go for a short meeting with our resident dog psychologist who will explore whether your aspirations and dreams match up with those of the animal. Then, there are substantial fees to pay for shots. Then," and she beamed, "then, you can rescue your new compadre and take him to his forever home." She handed Mitch a form on a clipboard. "Fill it out.

After approval," she added, "you get him. You realize that we have neutered him?"

"What's the neuter business do? How painful was it?"

"They removed his reproductive organs. We gave him a local."

"You mean they cut off his balls?" Mitch said. "But he's always gotten his jollies as a solitary performer. I don't think he would be getting it on with other dogs."

"We do this for every dog. Then, we don't have a lot of other strays to place."

"But doesn't that make him sort of…I mean…less of a man?"

The shelter worker smirked. "He's not a man, he's a dog."

"So now he won't get to enjoy doggy type fun-filled nights."

"Sir, dogs don't have romantic sleepovers. Coitus is usually over in seconds."

Mitch shrugged and filled out the form. The receptionist escorted him into an office. A pleasant gray-haired woman in a green kennel jumpsuit showed him a chair. "I'm Lucy, the shelter director and canine psychologist." She read through Mitch's scrawled answers while he sat in a nervous state.

"I see you live alone?"

"Yes."

"On a boat?" she asked.

"Yes."

"You note you had all different pets when you were young."

Mitch lied like a politician. "Oh yeah. Flipper. Cujo. Lassie. White Shadow. Family dogs. Cats. Hamsters. Turtles. Snakes. Guppies. Even an ant farm."

But you haven't had so much as a parakeet in the last ten years."

"True, but I was traveling a lot. Now that I have a city job, and am part of a startup over at MINSY, I won't be moving anywhere. I've settled down."

"Have you seen the dog?"

"I actually dog sat for Chipper. Did that several times during the few last months. We get along really well. I even brought his favorite biscuits," Mitch said.

"You know, of course, why he is here. He's been under quarantine after he bit his former owner's new companion."

"He bit Hunter?" Mitch smiled as he tried to visualize this. "That's great news. Where?"

"In a very sensitive area. Beyond that, I won't say. The bite required a hospital stay."

Mitch laughed out loud and pointed to his pants. "He really bit him there?"

"I'm afraid I can't say. But it was severe." And she cracked a tiny smile.

"Holy shit, that's great," Mitch said. "Well, don't worry, I can handle Chipper."

"Okay, let's go see the dog." They walked into a noisy kennel with a row of cages. Chipper was lying in the back of his enclosure, making a racket while licking himself. He jumped up and wagged his tail when he saw Mitch.

Lucy smiled. "It's so cute. He remembers you. You guys are simpatico."

"Chipper never forgets."

"Okay," she said, and opened the door to the cage. Chipper leaped into Mitch's arms and licked his face. Mitch pulled a biscuit from his pocket and Chipper licked his lips. Mitch's lips.

It was a done deal.

On the way back to the marina, the first stop was CrittersPlanet, a voluminous pet superstore filling up one corner of a floor in a failed and empty Sears building. Chipper rode in the shopping cart, barking softly in approval as Mitch splurged for a dog bed, canned chicken parts, a leash and satin collar, liver-flavored treats, tennis balls, an inflatable female terrier toy, and a dog-sized Greek fisherman's cap.

By Sunday night, Hope Stinger had packed up her belongings in Napa and snuck back to Vallejo. Her wine country blowup with cable star Hunter Callahan had become a national tabloid circus. The tragedy of their first night together marred her confidence like a hot frying pan scorching her soul. But when she had learned from doctors that his injuries would have kept him from producing a family—that settled it. He was out of the equation.

She was in city hall on Monday morning, eager to get back on the job. Everyone gave her a warm smile, saying they were delighted to see her return, and commiserated when the mayor told lies about Chipper wandering off in Napa. They all agreed that the email Dear John message from Hunter was totally classless. She went straight to her office and took to the pile of documents stacked in the in-box. On top was a scrawled note from Lieutenant Commander Noah Merrydale. "When things settle down, I'd love another karaoke night at Padre Jaime's." She smiled. Maybe that would work out.

Still, it was hard to concentrate. Nothing had changed and everything had changed. While at her desk, she looked at Chipper's unused dog bed over by the wall. *Where is the little fellow?* She wondered. *I miss the slurping sound from the dog bed. Will he forgive me for abandoning him at the pound?*

She called her assistant into the office.

"Lettie, you are the best."

"Thank you, Madame Mayor."

"You are like my vice-mayor. I couldn't run this city without you."

"That's kind of you to say. So, tell me, your honor, what do you need this time?"

"Lettie. It's a special assignment for you. One that is very hush-hush."

"Don't worry, Mayor, my lips are sealed. Is it zoning? Budget shortfalls? Dirty campaign tricks? Rile up my Fil-Am constituencies. Back door fundraising?"

"Lettie, I am so missing my dear Chipper."

"I could guess that was going to happen."

"I want you to find out who adopted Chipper from the shelter." The Mayor paused as a tear moistened her eye. "And Lettie, ask that person if he would consider returning him to his rightful owner."

"Will do, Ma'am."

"And do this with utmost discretion. I've got to see if he'll take me back."

"Yes, Mayor. I'm on it. I'm sure Chipper hasn't forgotten his home."

"Then you'll do what you have to do. I want that dog back."

"I'll take care of it Ma'am."

"You won't take no for an answer?"

"That's not an option."

"Okay, then I know you know what you've got to do."

Hope was upbeat but knew this was not going to be easy.

Chipper never forgets.

16

Exultation Over Chipper

"Mayor's Mutt Home At Last" screamed the *Times-Herald's* full banner headline. "Mayor's Aide Rescues Vallejo's First Dog From Dognapper's Pickup."

The poignant tearjerker photo on the front page featured the beaming Mayor cradling Chipper in her arms. The press run with that juicy item sold out quickly at supermarket checkouts, liquor stores, tire repair shops and the few non-vandalized street newspaper stands.

The story went on to say that Lettie Melendez, the Mayor's chief of staff, had spotted Chipper riding in the passenger seat of a beat-up maroon Toyota pickup as the truck crossed Vallejo. She told police she followed it to a parking lot, watched the driver get out and go into an adult video store, and then broke the window to rescue a grateful little Chipper.

Mitch went ballistic.

First he called the *Times-Herald* reporter, cursing and demanding a correction. "I'm not a dognapper. I'm the victim of a governmental dognapper. Last week, I rescued the Chipper from the pound where the Mayor had abandoned him. The dog is legally mine. Now, her Gestapo agents have broken into my pickup and stolen my pooch."

"Um. We'll have to check that out. The Mayor told us Chipper ran off one night in Napa."

"The Mayor is lying," Mitch said.

"Or you could be. I mean, whom should I believe? The chief executive of a major city or a low level city marina bait shop worm scooper?"

"I have the legal pooch adoption papers if you'd like to see them. I have a photo of Chipper and myself taken by the Humane Society when I rescued the dog."

"You could have faked those."

"And I want other retractions. My truck is not a clapped out old Toyota. It's in perfect condition. Except where the mayor's thugs smashed my passenger side window. And I wasn't going to the adult porn shop. I was headed to the nearby medical offices. My anxiety was acting up after reading crappy, sensational stories like this."

"Thank you, Mr. Wellborn, we'll consider your objections."

Then Mitch called the Mayor's office. Hope picked up. "Mayor Hope Stinger. What can the city of Vallejo do for you?"

"This is Mitch. I want my dog back."

"Your dog? It's my dog."

"You walked away from him at the pound. I rescued little Chipper before he was to be executed. Before those murderers put him to sleep. They were escorting him to the gas chamber when I intervened."

"I never dropped him at the pound. He ran away. The Humane Society truck must have picked him up. The pound never called me. However, I do appreciate you taking care of him until I could recover him from your dognapper's pickup. He's home now and I'm going to be gracious and not press charges. Bless you. Mitch. Also, you should be careful. If you push this dog ownership business any further, you might stimulate a review your probationary job status. Or, if the story quiets down, I could make you the permanent assistant harbormaster."

"So, I get the sense that you are threatening my position with the city?"

"No, just looking at the budget reality of staff positions for Vallejo. We need to cut a few useless jobs and we are looking at the lowest level ones. That's you."

"So it's Chipper or my job?"

"I never said that," the Mayor said

"Well, then you might consider that I know for a fact that before the special night in Napa when you went to hook up with Foxie news glamor boy, you spent the entire afternoon is the arms of a certain Coast Guard Lieutenant Commander with a biblical name."

"That is not true."

"It is. You know it is. I have photos. I was outside his house on Butte Street and have pictures of you coming and going. When you emerged into the sunshine, you were wearing a sailor boy sundress, and you were barefoot carrying your sandals, and you were hiding behind a huge pair of dark glasses. Your hair was a mess and you walked funny, like you were bowlegged, while leaving through the side door."

"So what. I was there to discuss the sunken mini-sub," the Mayor said.

"Get real. I don't think your family values backers will believe that."

"Well, you might have a hard time convincing people."

"Not with the pictures once they go up on social media."

"All right. All right. I'll tell you something I never told anyone. That afternoon tryst was a one-time deal. I wanted one last fling before I pledged my loyalty to my future husband. So, do you understand?"

"Wow, that breaks my heart. I think we can work on a plan to get little Chipper back to me. As a favor, I've recorded this conversation today. You know, as they say, for training purposes only. If things don't happen, you will be in a legal pickle, Madame Mayor."

Hope was steamed. "Forget it Mitch."

His response was quick. "See you in court."

Solano County Superior Court Judge SueAnn Hamm strode into her courtroom in formal judicial robes. The bailiff announced the case "Wellborn versus Stinger." Hamm dreaded another helter-skelter day in this so-called Mediation Court. No attorneys were allowed. The litigants present their own cases. She expected the usual—bitter feuds, arguments, name-calling, and shouting matches.

Judge Hamm peered up over her glasses and then grimaced. Standing before her was Mitchell Wellborn, the plaintiff, requesting custody of a terrier named Chipper, and next to him was the well-known defendant, Vallejo's mayor Hope Stinger, who argued the dog was hers.

The pooch in question, Chipper, lolled in a dog bed in the back of the courtroom.

"All right, you two, court is in session. You both agreed to the rules. After you finish arguing and be-littling each other, I will rule and that's final. Think of me as Judge Judy. I get to say what I want and there are no appeals."

Both nodded.

"Mr. Wellborn, you may go first."

"Thank you, Judge. On October seventh, I adopted Chipper at the Vallejo Benicia Humane Society. I have the papers and a photo taken that day to prove it. They told me that the Mayor had dropped the dog off, calling him a pest. Then on October eighth, in Vallejo, one of her Gestapo city servants broke my car's window to steal my dog. Now, she won't give Chipper back. She also is my boss and threatened to eliminate my position as the city's Assistant Harbormaster if I made trouble. I have a recording of her threat. Want to hear it?"

"Not yet, Mr. Wellborn."

The judge scanned the page. "I suppose that the

little fellow slurping away in on the back bench is the animal?"

"Yes it is."

Chipper was grooming, a pastime that grew noisier as he picked up the pace. His chain link leash collar began to smack against the wooden seat, banging faster and faster, the slurp louder and louder, the collar whacking away, building in tempo until it culminated in a shrieking satisfied canine moan that echoed through the old plaster courtroom.

Judge Hamm was becoming angry. "Can you get the dog to stop that?"

"It's his way of coping, your Lord," Mitch said.

"Before I go any further with this, I want that noisy dog out of here."

"You cannot do that, your Honor," Hope said. "Chipper is a service dog."

"And what service has he been trained for?"

"Companionship."

"And where did his training take place?"

"Well, he hasn't actually been trained professionally," Hope added.

"Then he's not legally a service dog."

"But he provides companionship."

"So does a pet walrus. But that doesn't make him a service dog."

Mitch piped up. "Your majesty, he has an official service dog collar."

"And where did you get that?" the Judge asked.

Mitch held up a paper receipt. "I bought it at CrittersPlanet. It cost nine bucks."

"Mr. Wellborn. You could buy yourself a collar but that doesn't make you a service dog. Get that neurotic animal out of here."

Mitch was testy. "Judge. Really. Neurotic? Not by a long shot. In fact, ejecting him might provoke a lifetime of disturbed sexuality. He'll go mental and need therapy. He already has enough doggy problems caused by living underfoot the Mayor, the woman who discarded him, who abandoned him."

"Mayor Stinger, I would like to hear your side."

"Well, your Honor, Chipper has always been my dog. I submitted a series of articles from the *Times Herald* showing Chipper and me at many public functions. One night, while I was visiting my future husband in Napa, Chipper ran away. I was heartbroken. By the time I got to the pound, this cretin Wellborn had already swooped down and absconded with him."

"That's all you have to say?"

"That's it. Chipper is my dog and I am going to keep him." She turned to Mitch. "You aren't getting him, you crude, lying worm scooper."

"Worm scooper? You had to decide between your loving dog and hide the weenie with a celeb, so you gave up the pooch. Remember, Chipper never forgets."

"Well, at least I am getting some sex, you eunuch."

The judge slammed down her gavel. "Enough, you two. Madame Mayor, according to the documents submitted by Mr. Wellborn and with affidavits from the Humane Society, you did indeed bring the dog to the pound, hand him to the staff, and call him "so much a pest." So you are lying about that. And then, in a remorseful mood, you must have asked your assistant to break into Mr. Wellborn's truck to steal the dog from him. And finally, you threatened his job. Is this accurate?"

The Mayor bit her lower lip. "Yes, Judge. Well, all that sort of happened. But I was distraught. I had just been through a wrenching emotional catastrophe."

"You mean your plans for a future with that cable news teevee personality?"

"Yes."

"I know your story because it was in the tabloids at the Safeway checkout counter. I don't buy that trash but I might have thumbed through one while in line. From your tearful account, I guess little Chipper really nailed your intended. Chomped on the family jewels. A lot of men deserve this. Certainly my ex-husband would have learned from getting his grapes in a grinder. But that doesn't excuse your actions, Madame Mayor, some of which border on criminal."

Judge Hamm shuffled the papers in front of her. "Now, I am ready to rule. It's a unique case because both of you have ownership rights. Therefore, for the dog's well being, I am going to order joint custody. That's right. You two antagonistic people will have to work together. From this point on, consider yourselves the legal co-parents of little Chipper. Through sickness and health, you two need to cherish each other and strive to keep the other happy. Sit down and produce a schedule of custody and visits. Madame Mayor, you must also give me your word that you will protect Mr. Wellborn's job with the city. So, hammer out that custody schedule by Friday or the obnoxious self-pleasuring terrier goes back to the Humane Society. Understood?"

"Is that it, your Lord?" Mitch asked. "Who gets him today? Mom or dad?"

"Oh, for chrissakes, Mr. Wellborn. I guess dad for the first week. Then mom for the second. And so on."

"Thank you, your Honor" the Mayor said.

The judge slammed down the gavel. "And get that dog out of here."

17

Hope Completes the Package

Settling Chipper's future had eased Hope's anxiety. That is, until she arrived at city hall in the morning.

It was déjà vu. A haze that was clearly marijuana smoke filled her office. So did the five "Don't Smoke My Vallejo" activists lounging on chairs and the couch along the wall. They were posing for another group shot for the *Times-Herald*.

"How do you like the air quality today, Madame Mayor?" a protestor asked sarcastically. He was burning weed in her metal wastebasket.

"Come on, everybody. Put the fire out. You've made your point again." Hope began opening windows. "My god. You certainly aren't very creative. This BS is getting old."

"But your processing plant has had three poison air releases so far."

"Look, there's another side. The plant brings in sixty much-needed jobs. That's sixty paychecks for our struggling city. And the funky air alerts were always cancelled right away. No one has been poisoned."

"Well, it's bound to happen," a protestor huffed. "It is our destiny."

The sheriff's deputies arrived, used an extinguisher to put out the fire, and dragged the activists out the side door.

"We'll be back," yelled the last one. "We'll be back because one day, the whole city will be whacked by fumes from the plant. You'll see."

Actually, Hope thought the festering marijuana brouhaha, with its volatile headlines and Internet notoriety, was just a distraction. She needed instead to focus on the monetary return from the El Gordo mini-sub explosion. This week, the lifelike Mermaid dolls were due from the Chinese factory. The shipments of Taiwan made models of the mini-sub El Gordo were already on sale at the ferry terminal.

A sculptor's life-size bronze statue of Jaylyn, her arms swept back as if she was careening through the air, was now installed on the walkway along Shoreline Park. It was wildly popular and inspired tourists and locals to spread their arms back to imitate Jaylyn's wingspan, and then take thousands of selfies.

Film rights were adding to the treasury, but even more crucial to Vallejo's dollar needs was the two-year waiting list for a chance to be cannonballed on the Mermaids Flight ride. That attraction would open on November third, the day after the Re-Sail Festival. Despite the total lack of scientific data backing up the rumor of rapturous erotic experiences, eager women from across America ponied up the fifty-dollar on-line reservation fee for their turn, hoping that it might take them places their husbands, boyfriends or other partners couldn't. Vallejo was cleaning up, pocketing fifty percent of the two hundred dollar fare for each ride.

Today Hope would concentrate on one last item to wrap up the revenue package. This required a foray into unfamiliar territory—producing music. The Mayor had commissioned the local Delta country western band the Lowlife Squats to write a syrupy ballad that would become an iconic brain worm to market the Mermaid Flight experience. They had invited Hope to a recording session at the remote studio later this morning.

Hope knew her look would be crucial. She changed into a down home outfit of stretch jeans, cowboy boots and a torn and ripped Merle Haggard T-shirt. The Estuary Recording Studio was on Grizzly Island in the Delta, about an hour's drive. When she arrived, she met the band in the front office and hugged each of the Lowlife Squats. The Squats were well known locally but only played in dive bars and social gatherings now. They were on the second draft of the lyrics.

A well-worn leather couch stretched across the back of the Estuary's control room. Hope plopped down next to Bald Chad, the band's long-time keyboard player and manager. She squeezed his hand and gushed, "This is so, so exciting. I so loved the first draft of the lyrics you emailed to me. Now you said you'd come up with some more really explosive ones. So, I want you to entertain me. Be awesome."

Chad handed the mayor the newly rewritten song. It had been toned down and re-shaped as a tearjerker, stealing the tune from an amalgam of several old country hits. "We added a bit of raunch to make it memorable," he suggested. "Let me play it to give you an idea."

"Oh, so do it," Hope said.

Chad picked up an acoustic guitar and began.

"Never knew I was destined for the sky
Never guessed little Jaylyn would fly.
But when I landed feet first in that cold, cold water
I was shredding the borders of ecstasy.

Got a blast in my ass and am flying alone,
Stirring a crazy orgasmic world.
Orgoplasm Airlines. What a way to fly.

On the channel bottom I rolled in the muck,
Hoping I wasn't going to get stuck.
But the moment I broke up through the surface,
I throbbed with my ride's hidden purpose.

"Got a blast in my ass and am flying alone,
Stirring a crazy orgasmic world
Orgoplasm Airlines. What a way to fly.

The shudders rocked me from head to feet
The pleasure made my boyfriend obsolete

I'm never going back to the olden ways
I crave for my pleasure Al Fredo."

Hope swallowed hard. This thorny rough draft needed editing on the spot. Lettie would know what to do. Her other advisers were not here. Still, she took Chad's hand in hers. "Could the band soften the "blast in my ass" part a bit? Come up with something else. And," she added, "it's not Al Fredo. You mean al fresco."

Chad whistled through his teeth. "I don't know. The old version has the raunchy bits that'll make it a big hit."

"Well, not everyone in city government will like this. Let's reword it a bit. How about "Got a blast from behind and am flying alone?""

The age-old dilemma of artistic freedom was under the gun. Would Bald Chad stand his ground and defend his art or cave in for the money?

His answer was immediate. "Sure," he said. "We can do that."

Chad and the band went back into the studio to record the new tracks. Hope headed outside for a breath of air. Chad's twenty-one-year old son Garrett was standing on the wooden deck, smoking while gazing out over tall stands of Delta salt grass. He was handsome, dark-haired with a pony-tail, slim hipped and skinny like his dad. "Want a hit?" he asked, offering her a fragrant joint he was nurturing.

"Sure," Hope said, inhaling an inordinate volume

of the potent smoke. Grass was only an occasional recreation for her.

"So, you're the famous mayor. You are all my dad has talked about lately."

"That's me, Garret. So what's he been saying? All good, I hope."

"Says you are smart, foxy, and easy to work with."

"Well, I'm flattered. Not everyone thinks that. But, how about you? I hear you are quite the musician. Why aren't you in the band?"

"They're old farts. Playing yesterday's music. I grew up watching my dad struggle to make money and raise myself and my two brothers. We never had a cent. He keeps playing because he loves music. Right. But he's broke all the time. Completely broke. Right now I'm in two bands in San Francisco. We tour. We rake in the dollars. I'm up here today because I love this Estuary studio. You look out at the water and you can't see another building. That takes me to a really sweet place."

Hope was attracted to this kid. He smelled like leather. She reached out and touched his wrist. "Want to go for a little walk?"

"Sure."

The two stepped down off the wooden deck and poked along a narrow path through the field grass and shrub. The sun beat down warm. Conversation had ceased. Hope took off her boots and walked barefoot in the cool sand. When they were out of sight of the studio, Hope fantasized they were miles from any civilization. They kept walking for ten minutes, saying nothing.

"This is so beautiful. So raw," she said finally.

"Yeah, I'm in another space when I'm out here." Garrett had turned to face her. "I feel so alive. So feral." He had moved his hand onto her shoulders and was beginning to massage the back of her neck.

Hope was getting shudders, but she heard her cell phone text tone. There was a message from Chad.

"New tracks are down. Mix in five minutes. Can U get here?"

Hope shrugged. "They're ready." She reached into her purse, pulled out a brush and began to straighten up her hair. "Well, this is disappointing but business calls. Do you like karaoke? Maybe we can meet up another time?"

"Maybe," Garrett said. "Don't know about karaoke but I'd like a second chat."

Back in the studio, the musicians and the engineer played back various mixes. Everyone finally agreed on one that was best. There were high fives all around.

Chad approached the delighted Hope. "I'm doing a keyboard gig this week at the Frog Pond Java Hut on Georgia Street. Six to nine. Drop by and I'll play your special requests?"

"I'll check out my schedule," Hope said, "and if there's no city business, you'll see me there.

The newly crafted country ballad made the front page in the *Times-Herald*. The newspapers music critic reviewed a copy, calling it "a crass exploitation of a social disaster with juvenile lyrics and a poached melody." She also said she thought these deficiencies would make it a solid hit.

That story ran in the Arts section beside a more bewildering item from the Delta. A *Times-Herald* reporter and photographer did a photo essay on two ceramic toilets, sitting out in the open in a field on Bethel Island. They had become a tourist attraction.

The outdoor commodes were leftovers from a summer community development project sponsored by the United Nations High Commission on Squalor. The goal had been to build new bathrooms for a downtrodden marina on a backwater channel. It seems the U.N. workers had completed the plumbing part of the project and then staged what they called a Loo Palooza party. They brought in photographers and paid the local residents to take turns posing fully dressed on the new toilets. The photos went out on Facebook and Instagram. Within a week, the prints of the Delta johns with smiling locals posing atop appeared in billboard-sized posters in the United Nations headquarters building lobby in New York City. Bethel Island's toilets became a national phenomenon.

In true Delta fashion, events went downhill after that. The next day, the Squalor crew loaded up their RV and split, leaving the freestanding toilets behind. Weeds grew around the site. A local artist, and not a very good one, painted flowers on the ceramic stools. When the word got out, visitors touring the Delta began taking selfies sitting on the art installation.

Finally, the Bethel Island locals had had enough of the crowds. They descended on the open-air thrones with sledgehammers and pry bars. When they had finished, they had demolished the monuments left by the United Nations High Commission on Squalor.

The destruction was a blessing.

The tourists stopped coming.

The newspaper tried to contact the woman who headed the U.N. project, a Krista Jönsdöttir. But she had disappeared.

Life in the Delta chugged on, once again undisturbed.

On Thursday, when Hope finally got around to dropping in on Chad's three-hour music gig, the Frog Pond Java Hut coffeehouse was nearly deserted. The long, narrow, high-ceilinged room with the polished red espresso machine and dessert cold case at the front was fragrant with a pleasant coffee aroma but eerily quiet. A poster by the door announced the week-long three-hour music stint from six to nine. No cover.

Ten tables stretched in a line from the street door to the back wall. Nearest the front, four men had spread backpacks around a table, and two were focused on the Chinese board game of Go. At the other end, Chad sat alone at the piano on a riser, playing and singing into a microphone on a stand.

Hope and her assistant Lettie breezed in and

walked to the back table nearest the piano. Both women sat facing Chad, no more than six feet away. Hope had dressed for a coffeehouse look, wearing a black sweater, leather pants and dark glasses. Lettie had a jean jacket and black stretch pants.

"Thanks for inviting me," Lettie whispered. "I don't get out much. This should be fun."

"Well, you're also here to help me decide something. Chad is so sweet and in pretty good shape. He's tall and I've told you I sort of got the hots for him. But my friends who had hooked up with musicians say it's nothing but misery, especially with someone who plays in bars and clubs for many years and whose career has never really gone anywhere. So, I'm really on the fence about so taking another step."

"I'll be happy to give you whatever advice I can," Lettie said.

Chad was in the middle of a song. When he saw the women sit down, he finished it with a flourish and smiled toward them. Hope clapped loudly but the Go players at the other end of the room continued in a loud conversation.

Hope turned and gave them a dirty look.

"What's their problem? That's really rude," she said. "Lettie, go back and tell them to at least acknowledge the musician."

"They're busy with their game."

"But they could clap."

"Hope, this is your job as Mayor. Go back and tell them yourself."

"Okay, I will." Hope strode across the room and approached the game players. "Excuse me," she said. "I don't mean to interrupt your little checkers game but you guys should be more courteous to the musician. It's tough to play to an empty room. Why don't you at least acknowledge his artistry with a little applause?"

A bearded player with his back to the piano responded without looking up at her. "Why should we? We're busy."

"That's rude," Hope said.

"Lady, I don't mind what the loser plays. He can do what he wants. Besides, we aren't playing checkers. It's called Go. Now why don't you go? Go to hell."

"Young man, you are pissing me off. That's not the true Vallejo Spirit."

"Ma'am, we're not from Vallejo. And we don't give a shit about your spirit."

Hope walked back to her chair. "Assholes," she muttered.

Chad was beginning his rendition of a movie tune, *New York, New York*. "Start spreading the news, I'm leaving today…"

One of the Go players made a surprise move. The other player and the two watchers let out a cheer. Hope jumped up.

"All right. Can't you guys keep it a little quieter."

The bearded player facing Hope gave her the finger.

Chad continued…"Your small town blues…"

Hope turned and raised her hand. "Chad. Chad. Hold it. Hold it. Hey, that's the problem. That's why there's no one here. Nobody wants to hear those ancient songs?"

Chad stopped and faced her. His expression was deadpan. "And what would you like me to play?"

"How about El Paso. The country ballad. You know, Marty Robbins, "out in the west Texas…""

"That's not more recent and I don't know the lyrics very well."

"That doesn't matter. It's a big favorite in the karaoke bars. Try it for me."

Chad banged out a few notes and then began playing the tune. He sang "Out in the West Texas town of El Paso, I fell in love with a Mexican maiden…"

"Stop. Stop," Hope shouted. "That's not right. It's 'Down in the West Texas town of El Paso, I fell in love with a Mexican girl."

"Well, Hope, give me a break. I told you I didn't know the song very well."

"Why not. Everyone I know who sings karaoke knows that one. But I guess you don't."

"No."

"Okay, you play it and I'll sing it. Give me the microphone."

"No. This is my gig. I'm here to play and sing, not bring up volunteer vocalists."

"No, I only so want to sing one. I sing all the time at Padre Jaime's karaoke night. Besides, the assholes playing checkers won't be listening—only the barista."

"No. I'll do another. One that I know."

"I mean, why won't you let me sing?"

"Because it's my gig."

"Oh, so it's your gig. Well, you're gigging for an empty church. Bucko. You need a vocalist. If you ever are going to make any hard coin doing this. I mean, how do musicians survive? I mean, you've got to monetize these opportunities. How long have you been at this and you still aren't sucking in an audience. And look at the empty tip jar. It's got spider webs in it."

One Go player shouted from the front. "Will you guys shut up. We're trying to concentrate."

"Shut up yourself," Hope yelled. "I'll call the police if you criminals make another sound." She turned to Lettie and spoke softly. "I'm thinking this is a disaster. Let's get out of here. Do you have any bills for the tip jar?"

"No. Just a roll of quarters I got for my laundromat."

"Give me a bunch." Hope dropped the ten quarters into the empty beer pitcher. They rattled noisily.

"Change? Only change?" Chad said. "How about some bills?"

"No way," said Hope. "You need to expand your repertoire." *And your life*, she thought. This was the watershed—her momentary infatuation with the music world was over. Done. Maybe she had been taken in by his beard or his sorrowful eyes. But, hey. Tonight was her cold shower. Now, she knew there was no way she would ever, ever hook up with a musician. Why, he'd be penniless forever and she'd have to bring in the dough.

"Ready, Lettie?"

"Yes I am, Madame Mayor." Lettie seemed disappointed.

"Yeah. No use sitting here listening to crappy music. I'm too far down the line to be spinning my wheels. This isn't going to work."

Chad watched them leave and turned back to the piano.

18

Maggie and MINSY

"You gonna eat the rest of that?" Valerie stabbed her fork in the direction of a muffin leftover on Maggie's plate. Her hand was shaking.

"Yes, I am. I told you before, I don't share my food. Buy you own, Val."

This interloper's familiarity was brash—after all, she only arrived in Vallejo days ago. Maggie was beginning to wonder how this strange, nervous woman could still be a working agent. Or, if she really was one? Or, whom she really worked for?

They finished their poached egg breakfasts in silence. Maggie asked "So, tell me what you found out about the U.N. program in Serenity?"

"Well, they had one on Bethel Island. Not Serenity. The whole thing was a paradox. They spent money to reduce squalor in the world's richest country. On glossy Bethel Island. And the project ended half-finished. They never completed the bathrooms. In the final report, there was a footnote about Serenity and only one mention for Krista Jönsdöttir. So, this makes me wonder—was she really on staff for the U.N.? I mean, why would this older Krista person be on a college age project?"

"But should we worry?" Maggie asked. "I mean, their project is over. She's gone. She seemed genuine to me. Basic do-gooder helping out in a blighted area?"

"Could be genuine, but she didn't fit in. I don't like that. I think she's a floater. Comes out of nowhere. Disappears. A ghost agent. And the more checking I do, the more I doubt her story. I'll keep on top of it."

"Anything new on Carver?" Maggie said.

"Well, he's been gone three days now. The lack of any contact is unsettling. We might begin a search. Get out that map."

Maggie unfolded a page with the layout of deserted buildings on the MINSY property, and began to highlight a few she thought were important.

Then she stopped. She stared over Valerie's shoulder.

Two men with shaved heads loitered in the diner's cramped entryway bar. "The goons from my photo shoot are over there," Maggie whispered. "I'm sure of it. Check out the one with a bandage on his nose."

Valerie spun to get a look. The pair chatted, waiting for coffees to go.

After a minute, she turned back. "I know them. Those are mercenary scum who work with arms dealers in Marseille. They were speaking French."

"What would they be doing here?"

"Good question. From what I gather, this part of

Vallejo is just a bunch of boat works and the Coast Guard station and yard, Of course, a French connection might be part of this and these are sleepers working with crime gangs in southern France. They might be after the warhead."

"So, what's the big deal about this nosecone? I still don't get it. It's forty years old. That's Stone Age technology. Yesterday's potatoes. Why now?"

"We believe the dissident scientists' group found an out-of-the-box way to deliver non-lethal gases. That's technology certain countries would like to have even now. And the thugs by the register are real. So they are working for somebody. And, don't be shocked, but it makes me think Carver might be running their op."

"What do you mean? Carver might be involved?"

"Before he left D.C., Carver was aging. He looked rundown. Some questioned his ability to function at a high level. They thought he had become a careless agent who might endanger others. So they cut him loose. And then, after the torpedo came up, a wire tap last week caught him telling a source about a French op."

"What should we do?" Maggie asked.

"It's hard to make sense with Carver dropping from sight. The longer he is out of touch, the greater the possibility that he is calling the shots. By that I mean, leading us by our noses. We've got to counter strategize. But right now, I'm keeping an eyeball on those two."

Valerie watched as the men paid for their coffees,

then walked across the parking lot and climbed into a beat up Chevy Suburban. She wrote down the license.

"This might be upticking the timetable. We'll have to move faster. I don't like unknowns going after the same hard target."

Maggie started to gather her things. "I'm heading back to the Duck. Come with me and I'll make you a copy of the MINSY map."

On the way to her boat, they could see Mitch walking along B dock. A small dog with a Greek fisherman's hat followed at his heels.

Maggie yelled. "Finally got a date, Mitch?"

"It's Chipper. You know the mayor abandoned him. I just got joint custody."

"With Stinger?" Maggie yelled.

"Yeah, it's all legal."

"You're kidding. So you have to be civil with each other. How's that going to work out?"

"Yeah, so far, so good. She's not so bad. Has been real nice to me. We need to pamper each other if we want to keep little Chipper. Only hope we don't spoil him."

Inside the Duck's cabin, Maggie was anxious. She paced. "Val, this spy loyalty. I mean it's weird. Whose side is anyone on? Even makes me wonder about you."

"Me? I'm not offended if you question my motives. You don't know me from Adam. I could just be some agency leftover freelancing on a new op. Maybe I am."

There was silence. Finally, Maggie shrugged. "So.

I sort of have to trust you. We need to move forward."
Maggie handed Valerie a copy of the map. "There
are hundreds of empty buildings on the old MINSY,
but I think number 1617 might be our best bet. At
least for a first foray."

"We need to get started tonight. You say it's building 1617. You know, I wish Carver were all we were
looking for. I'll tell you now there's another location
we need to find. A hidden lab. We've got work to do.
I'm glad we are getting off the dime."

19

Trolling the Base

At sunset, thin clouds spread a hazy canopy across the darkening sky. A fuzzy fingernail moon rose in the east. Maggie and Valerie drove through the desolate layout of scattered workshops and warehouses, stopping finally at building 1617, a square, four-story office structure adjacent to the backs of nineteenth century coal sheds.

"Carver talked about this building," Maggie said. "It's next to the baseball field."

"Why would that matter?"

"He said that underground tunnels crisscrossed portions of MINSY. Sometimes the Navy didn't fill them in, but just built playing fields or parking lots on the surface. Occasionally, the Navy hid secrets in these tunnels and used non-descript buildings like 1617 as access points. Then, they had places the Soviet satellite cameras wouldn't recognize."

Dressed in dark sweats, they circled the boarded up derelict building, until they came to a plywood barricade covering a south side utility door. "I've got flashlights," Maggie said, "and I've been in this old wreck ten times already."

Maggie pried back one wooden panel and climbed across the opening. Valerie followed. The interior was a labyrinth of trash-strewn hallways reeking of mold. The flashlight beams splayed in surreal patterns down corridors and into barren rooms.

"Maggie, its just junk. It looks like they walked away from it yesterday. I'm still not sure what we will find here."

From an east-facing second floor window, they could see the coal sheds in the distance and the abandoned baseball park next to the building. Weeds covered its dirt infield. The cinderblock dugouts behind the foul lines were still there, reminders of a time when workers might play a friendly softball game after work.

"It's baseball," Valerie said. "Carver loved baseball. After work, he liked the night games in Baltimore. If he was going to meet an asset at night, and if he needed an open area and a private place that was easily recognizable, he'd find a place that had a ball-park."

"Such as this field?"

Valerie pointed her flashlight at the stairs. "We'll need to check it out. The field might be above an old tunnel. Maybe we'll find a way in, in the basement."

"Okay by me."

"We're looking both for signs of Carver and that hidden lab," Valerie said.

"I guessed there was something beside Carver. You wouldn't be here otherwise. Okay, to the basement," Maggie said

Downstairs, they found more discarded furniture and broken desk chairs scattered around. In a room filled with empty employee lockers, Maggie pulled a bank of them from the back wall, revealing a roughly cut opening in the wooden wall paneling. "Bingo," she said. "We'll need tools to get through that."

Back outside, they separately walked in the tangled weeds and trash on the ball field. Each inspected the foul lines, the backstop, crawled beneath the bleachers and sat on the splintery benches in the dugout.

Nothing.

Not a clue.

Not until Valerie focused on a crude air duct grating in the back wall of the semi-sunken dugout. It was large, about a meter square, and painted the same color as the wall. It appeared to have no connection for the baseball needs of the field.

"Omigod. I didn't notice that. Do you suppose?" Maggie pounded on the grating, making an echo deep within the earth. "Where could this lead?"

"We'd have to follow it to find out," Valerie said. "It could have vented the old tunnels."

"Can you get a teevee camera on a metal snake. They use them for sewers."

"No," Valerie said with a smile. "We need a young person to crawl in."

Maggie smirked back. "Oh no. Don't look at me. I'm not going in there. Maybe one of your local spook agents can be talked into slithering into that duct."

"Now, with cutbacks, there's no one in the office. And I'm not so well connected here on the west coast. So, how about a local?" Valerie asked.

"Maybe Mitch. He and his man cave buddies go on and on about breaking into almost every empty structure on MINSY. He's bragged about climbing into shafts all over the base. He calls it duct-diving."

"But he'll catch on to us," Valerie said. "That would remove our cover."

"Maybe not. Mitch isn't the sharpest tool in the shed. And remember, Carver fascinates him. He's even taking Carver's night class at the library. He'd do it if we were looking for Carver."

"Will he keep his mouth shut?" Valerie asked.

"If we have an airtight cover story."

The next morning, Valerie Beckett received a troubling message from the local FBI in her room at the nearby Holiday Inn Express.

"A janitor found Carver's personal cell phone near a drainage ditch behind the Navy museum on Mare Island property. We are attaching a list of the last calls on it. You'll probably want to check it out. Again, sorry we don't have more news."

Valerie texted Maggie. "Meet you at the Can in ten."

When Valerie arrived, Maggie was staring out a window at the marina. "I couldn't sleep. I worried about those French thugs."

"Well, there's more to worry about than those bruisers," Valerie said.

"What?"

"I am less concerned about Carver anymore. My instincts tell me Carver might be orchestrating events one step ahead of us. He could be working for an independent contractor. We need to be vigilant."

"You mean Mr. America, our own conservative Carver, is now against us?"

"Not against us. For himself. That's different than competing with us. Anyhow, they found his cellphone behind the museum on the old Navy Base. That's a tradecraft trick to throw pursuers off his scent."

"I thought he might come back to his boat," Maggie said.

"I bet it's gone somewhere."

Maggie dashed out the Can's waterside door. She scanned the alphabet docks for the *Doublecross*. Back inside, she reported to Valerie. "Don't see Carver's trawler right off. But Mitch could have moved it down the docks."

"I don't think you'll find it. My guess is that he's using it for a base of operations."

"Why would he work for the other side?"

"Paying debts. Carver owes a lot of people."

"Now, what do we do?"

"Well, I suppose it would help to find Carver's boat. He must have stashed it somewhere near here. It might be a lead to the lab and the warhead."

"Mitch is beta testing a GPS system for his startup MINSY company and has put what he calls a Findola marker on everyone's boat. It's a GPS reflector. It gives location and traces any movements. I'll ask him if he knows about Carver's boat."

"Before you do, I've got questions about your personal French past. How well did you know your father? This Lieutenant René Bobillot?"

"Never met my biological father. He transferred from Mare Island before I was born and may be living in France. Apparently he was quite the fertile playboy, knocking up single women all over the base. I know I have other half-sisters, including Promise, who lives up in the Delta."

"Well, Lieutenant Bobillot was suspected of being a hostile agitator. Our agents couldn't produce any real evidence. Then his temporary assignment ended, and he left. But the rumors of the rogue group continued."

"So the history is murky."

"You could say that. I'd like to find out if Carver had any dealings with your Lieutenant Bobillot then. For now, see if you can find out where Carver's trawler went. Then we'll go through that suspicious locker room door and follow the sports field air duct. Did you talk to Mitch about coming with us?"

Maggie shrugged. "Not yet. But I'll do it. I promise."

"Do that soon. We need him."

20

Ducts Diving

"Why should I?" asked Mitch. "Call someone who gives a shit."

Maggie had phoned, begging for help. "Because Carver may be in danger. And we think we are on the trail of the bad guys. You want to be on the hunt?"

"Not with you," Mitch said. "I mean, I like him. He fascinates me. His stuff at the library about espionage and spy craft is great, even if he occasionlly forgets things. I mean, he really is spot on."

"So, you'd love those classes to continue? Right? You'll have to find him first. Mitch, I'm putting you on the speakerphone. Valerie is here with me."

Valerie joined in. "Mitch, you know I've worked with Carver for years, and I think if we act now, we might find him alive. But I'm too old and Maggie is too bulky—we really need someone who is adept at spelunking in ducts."

"So, you need my muscle? My unique skills?"

"Yes, your highly toned, tough as nails set of muscles," Maggie added.

"And that's tonight?"

"Yeah."

There was a long pause. Maggie feared he would say no.

"All right. I'll do it for you, Mags. But first you have to agree this is payback for the city council award song fuckup," Mitch said. "Agree to forgive me and I'm in."

"I will forgive and forget the inane insult if you do this," she said. "I promise."

"I believe you. Deal, Mags."

In two hours, Valerie and Maggie hurried across the darkened ball field next to Building 1617. Mitch scooted behind them with a heavy backpack of tools. The three settled into the trash strewn third base dugout on the softball diamond.

Mitch whispered. "I've got bad news, ladies. I tried to locate Carver's trawler but it seems he swept the hull for bugs and found my GPS transponder. So right now, there's no electronic way to spot him."

"What else can we do to find the boat?" Maggie asked.

"The old way. I'll make some calls to local harbors and marinas." He opened the backpack. "Now, this duct is definitely not new. It looks over fifty years old. Something low budget to ventilate something below. Then, they built a ballfield over it. Now, tell me how far am I going into this duct?"

Before Valerie could answer, they heard conversations. "Quiet," Valerie said. "Don't move. We've got company."

Two dark figures walked outside the fence on the edge of the ball field. One was tall and thin, the other shorter and stockier. The pair kept up chatter before they disappeared behind building 1617. Maggie, Valerie and Mitch could hear the unmistakable sound of the plywood door barrier being pried back. Then, silence.

"They're inside," Maggie said. "What'll we do?"

"We wait," said Valerie. Flashlight beams moved from room to room in the deserted office tower. "I don't think they know where they are going. They are searching, like we did. Let's just keep doing what we are doing," Valerie said. "We'll keep an eye on the building."

Mitch was busy, using an aerosol spray lubricant to loosen the grating's rusty fasteners. The trio lifted the screen and put it aside.

The opening was three foot square, covered with black grime and shrouded in spider webs. The air was cold and smelled moldy. Mitch slipped into a set of coveralls, heavy gloves and plastic safety goggles, and turned on a light attached to a headband. He strapped a respirator mask across his face and tied a line to a caribineer on his waist, "I'm guessing a fresh air vent for the ancient coal shed tunnels. The lower brick walls might be over a hundred years old. Someone fashioned this outlet up here when they built the field. Wish me luck," he said. "I've got a phone with me and can do Facetime as long as there is a signal. But I doubt I'll have any bars deep in the bowels of this baby."

He clambered headfirst on his hands and knees into the vent, coughing loudly into the mask as he stirred up the dust. "God, it is a bloody mess in here."

Progress was slow. Maggie and Valerie could hear him cursing as he slithered through the grime and cobwebs.

"I'm climbing down a short ladder." Mitch's voice was becoming more distant. "Ouch. Goddamit. scratched myself on a screw or something. I'm crossing a grating that appears to be on the ceiling of an arched tunnel."

There was silence for a minute. They could still hear his voice without the phone.

"Found another grating. It's on a wall. It's screwed on tight from the other side. My headlight is shining into a large open part of another tunnel. Looks like someone has used it for something else. I'd say it's under the infield."

"Okay, tell us exactly what you can see," Valerie yelled.

"Well, looks like it was some sort of a shop setup. There are large worktables, a desk, a drafting board, and a drill press. That's all I can see from here."

"Anything else?"

"Not really. Except that it looks very deserted," Mitch said.

"Can you climb down in?" Valerie asked.

"I'm guessing too dangerous. This old brick is pretty shaky."

"Okay, then, start back. We're sure we know where the basement door is."

There were scraping noises, curses, and thumps as Mitch turned around and began crawling back along the duct. Then he stopped. "Ssssh. A door is opening."

Silence. For thirty seconds. Finally, he whispered. "Someone came down the tunnel below me and into this room. I'm going to wait and see what's going on."

Valerie and Maggie could hear talking. This went on for ten minutes as the intruders conversed while searching through old desks and workbenches.

In another thirty seconds, Mitch spoke. "They're gone. Okay, I'm on the move again."

A shuffling noise echoed in the duct. Then a loud cracking sound. Mitch sounded troubled. "Uh-oh. Oh shit. The brick ceiling to the room is giving way."

Mitch screamed. His tether went tight. Then the sound of bricks cascading to a cement floor echoed up through the duct.

Maggie gave Valerie a worried look. "Fuck. What do we do now?"

The wait seemed like forever.

Finally, Mitch's voice was distant but still audible. He was clearly in distress. "Oh, crap. I fell. Landed on my back. Hit my head. I'm lying on one of the tables in the room. In a pile of rubble and old bricks. It smells like mold. I'm in the dark."

"Can you move?" Valerie yelled.

"Not sure. My leg is all twisted and I am dizzy. I hope you can get some help down here."

"Okay. Try to stay awake. We'll keep up the conversation from here."

Maggie pulled out her cell phone. "There's one person who could help. She has a very keen interest in keeping Mitch out of trouble."

21
Old Fights

The Commander had finished organizing a stack of month-end reports on his desk at the Coast Guard yard. It was nearly eight and he would be off duty in a few minutes. He wasn't expecting a call.

"Hope. What's up?"

"Commander, how are you feeling this evening?"

"Tired and bored out of my skull with paperwork. But it is always a delight to talk with my Mayor."

"Commander, I need a favor," Hope said. "Urgently."

"What is it?"

"Are you off for the evening soon?"

"In about ten."

"Chipper's dad, Mitch, is in a fix."

"Chipper's dad?"

"Just a legal figure of speech."

"Go on."

"He's trapped. He was duct diving in a deserted Navy building on MINSY and now he's lying injured after he fell through the top of an old coal storage tunnel."

"Why not call the developer's security or the Navy.

They'll help."

"Well, it's a bit more complicated. He shouldn't be there. We don't want to get him in trouble. I was wondering if you could take some personal time and get some of your Coast Guard buddies to do a private search and rescue mission?"

"Hope, it's almost eight o'clock. What if he has broken bones? This is way beyond a friendly little favor."

"Commander. You are my only chance. If you don't want me to go through that dog custody anxiety again, and listen to me weep about Chipper, then this is the time to step up. Besides, I'd be very grateful. Grateful, yes."

"Okay. I think Petty Officer Nelson and Seaman Orr are around. Which building is it?"

"It's 1617. Go to the back. The west side. You'll meet Valerie Beckett and Maggie Trout at the entrance"

"Okay. I should be there in a half-hour."

"Thanks so much, Commander. I'm hoping that next week we might get together for another long talk about the weirdness that has just happened."

"I'd like that."

"How ya feeling, Wellborn?"

Mitch startled awake. He knew that voice. He opened his eyes to see a flashlight in the hands of the backstabbing Commander Merrydale, who was dressed in civilian clothes.

"What? Why is the Coast Guard here? In civvies?" Mitch asked.

"Chipper's mom begged me to retrieve his dad. Anything broken?"

"No, don't think so. My leg is twisted. And I really banged my head."

"Well," the Commander said with a snicker, "that shouldn't damage anything."

"Fuck yourself, Commander. I nearly lost my job because of your cheesy submarine. You knew it was junk."

"Easy, Wellborn. I'm here to get you out of this place without anyone knowing more about it." He asked Nelson and Orr to clean away the bricks.

"What if I don't want to give you the pleasure of saving me?"

"Your wishes don't matter. Would you rather go to jail for trespassing. I'm not doing a rescue because I like you. I'd just as soon not be doing this."

"What sort of a room did I land in?"

"Well, it's an old coal tunnel under the ball field. And someone had turned it into a workshop, with machinery in it. Tools, Lathes. Grinders. Welders."

"Did you see those two guys?"

"Which guys?"

"The two guys who were here before I crashed down onto this spot."

"No. No guys around. I think you fell about an hour ago."

Mitch was still dizzy. "So, I suppose you'll want my gratitude."

"I told you. I don't give a fuck about your gratitude. I'm doing this for other reasons."

"What?"

"Not saying." The Commander signaled to Nelson and Orr. "Let's move this pathetic trespasser out. Don't be gentle."

They produced a litter and set it beside Mitch, rolling him onto it. He flailed, struggling to get off. They grappled with him, strapped him down and carried him back to the basement of 1617 where they set it down. Mitch fell out at Maggie's feet. The Commander had a short chat with her and then took his men back into the workshop.

Mitch sat on the floor, rubbing his head.

"Wow. Are you a mess. I hope your rescuers don't start looking around," Valerie said. "They might find something that we are looking for."

"Did we find anything?" Mitch asked.

"Oh, we did, but I hope the Coasties here don't discover what that room holds. Anyhow, we are closer to the trail of Carver, if that's any consolation."

Maggie pulled Mitch to his feet, brushing away some of the brick dust in his hair and on his face. She put her arm around his shoulder and helped him stumble up the stairs and out of the building. "Hey," she said. "Thanks. I'll gather up your tools and drive you back to the Marina."

Readers of the *Times-Herald* were shocked the next day when a front-page headline announced "Trap Door's Secret Workshop May Have Been Found".

The story reported how Lieutenant Commander

Noah Merrydale and a Coast Guard team, on a rescue operation for an injured colleague, uncovered a hidden Cold War workshop and lab on the former U.S. Navy shipyard at Mare Island. Merrydale confirmed that SUBROC parts scattered around inside the workspace in the old coal storage tunnel led him to believe this could be the hideout of the rogue scientists known as Trap Door.

The item went on to say that the Navy was sending a team of investigators.

The fourth paragraph explained that Vallejo residents had known for years about a clandestine group called Trap Door but that no one had found their operational base or would confirm their authenticity. Commander Merrydale said the newly found workspace hadn't been touched in decades.

The story caused fury with the Navy brass. Why was the Coast Guard out rescuing lame-brained nutjobs who explore the miles of air passages abandoned on their former shipyard? MINSY had been theirs. Historically, it still had the Navy stamp. And why did Commander Merrydale make this announcement without consulting them? At least he hadn't given away the location. They were, yes, very interested in that group called Trap Door. And the hidden lab.

So was an old-time agent named Valerie, but she was ninety-nine percent sure this lab was a set-up, a clever decoy op of her most bitter rival.

22

Headed for Wingo

The phone rang at the Commander's desk. It was the Commandant of the Coast Guard.

"Commander Merrydale. I was proud when I heard the news that you and your station's team uncovered what could be the hidden Cold War Navy workshop where that treasonous anti-war cell of scientists fomented disobedience."

"Yes, sir. We're almost sure it was the underground Trap Door outfit. They were very careful to stay under the radar. Thank you, Sir."

"We are always happy to assist our brothers at the Navy. They've been hunting these vile dissidents for years. But, we found them. Still, no gloating."

"No, Sir."

"Be tactful and not smug. The Navy brass is stewing. Tell me. Was this in some sort of below ground tunnel?"

"Yes, Sir. An old unused coal storage tunnel. I have escorted a Navy team to the location and showed them the disguised entrance to the corridor and lab."

"Good job. Keep up the good work. And keep my office posted."

"Yes, Sir."

"Well, then, good show Commander." And the Commandant hung up.

All morning long, the Commander acknowledged congratulatory calls, texts, emails, high-fives and knuckle bumps from other Coasties. The Commander was confident that this would repair his career damage after the El Gordo disaster.

But there was little time to bask in the limelight. Within a half-hour, he would begin conducting a long scheduled tour of the Coast Guard's Station Vallejo for the Vallejo Mayor and two members of the city council.

Hope showed up in a sparkling white sailor dress, a blue nautical blazer and stiletto heels. She slathered herself in her never-fail Dahlia Desire moisturizer.

The Commander began his orientation in the operations area and had just finished running down the day's training schedule when a seaman motioned frantically for him to come to the door.

"Commander. A break-in in the yard."

"When?"

"Sometime in the last two hours. In the equipment bay where we keep the SUBROC."

"What did they take?"

"So far, it doesn't look like they took anything big. Maybe something from the SUBROC."

The Commander couldn't hide his agitation. He apologized to everyone, shook hands with the Mayor and the two council members and then quickly excused himself. "We'll have to finish this up later. We have an unexpected military emergency. Thanks for coming," and ran from the room.

A side door to the single-story garage equipment bay had been pried apart at the lock. Inside, at first glance, everything seemed to be in place.

Until he looked at the SUBROC.

It was still there. At least, most of it. Someone had used tools to crudely remove the forward collar that attaches a nosecone to the SUBROC.

"What the hell." the Commander said. "Why would anyone want the attachment collar? But that's what they must have come after."

Nelson looked up at the surveillance cameras. "It looks like they sprayed the cameras with black paint. It's a very professional job. We won't have any video of it."

"No. We don't. But maybe the marina next door has something outdoors. Check with that Wellborn fellow. Tell him it's an emergency. Tell him he owes me. See if you can identify who it was and where they went."

Chipper and Mitch were relaxing in the marina office when Nelson burst in. "The Commander needs a favor. There's been a break-in at the yard."

"Can I help?"

"The last hour of your surveillance video focused on the parking lot by the Coast Guard yard's maintenance shed? Can we look?"

"Sure. I'll call it up on this monitor." Mitch said.

He played it for Nelson. On the video, two men in dark clothes with a duffle slipped through the gate into the Coast Guard yard. In ten minutes, they were back out. They carried a heavy bag across the public parking lot to the Marina's waterside walkway. Another camera caught them heading down D dock to the end mooring. They threw the satchel onto the back deck of the trawler tied there.

"Shit," Nelson said. "They got away."

Mitch chuckled. "Not quite. I saw the trawler arrive earlier today and went out and used my startup's proprietary laser system to tattoo a GPS target on the hull." He zoomed into the video image. "Incidentally, that's Carver Pardon's Hatteras Trawler. The *Doublecross*. And Carver is at the helm. Looks like they jacked his boat with him on it. You may have a hostage situation."

Nelson looked grim. "That makes it tougher. Where did they go?"

Mitch pointed to a thick yellow line on the screen. "See, they left here, motored about ten miles west across San Pablo Bay, and then went up Sonoma Creek to the abandoned steamer port at Wingo Wharf. It's moored there now."

"Wingo Wharf. Thanks," said Nelson.

"Need any help?"

"No. We're the Coast Guard. We'll take it from here. Civilians should stay out of it."

23

The Missing SUBROC Collar

I must breathe through my eyes. Breathe through my nose. Inhale mindfully. For Commander Merrydale, the meditation gibberish taught at the U.S. military's Command College was finally making sense. This breathing focus made it possible to channel all his efforts toward the next step—the imminent confrontation with the suspects who stole the SUBROC nose collar and took a Vallejo boater hostage. He was crystalizing his homegrown three-step battle mantra—pursue, engage, arrest.

Merrydale sat motionless in the left command chair on the enclosed bridge of MLB 88666 Golden Gate. He had commandeered the boat, on temporary assignment to the Vallejo station, and shanghaied a pickup crew to accompany him. Petty Officer Nelson was acting as coxswain and sat beside him in the enclosed bridge. Seaman Orr was the boatswain. Now thirty minutes out of the Station Vallejo, they already had crossed the northern side of San Pablo Bay and arrived at their current location, the mouth of Sonoma Creek.

It was getting dark but action was imminent. For the Commander, this night mission would be special. A litmus test for his military mettle. He had spent most of his Coast Guard career stopping drunken pleasure boaters in the Delta and checking for life vests. Now, capturing these suspects after a firefight would finally give him a battle record that might advance his promotion.

But there was a hitch. MLB 88666 bobbed dead in the water at the mouth of Sonoma Creek, waiting for a flood tide that would guarantee more keel clearance going upriver. Their objective would be to retrieve the stolen nosecone collar of the SUBROC and possibly free the boat's owner, who now might be a hostage. He and his crew would soon fire up the diesels, holster their Sig Sauer's and head into the heart of darkness.

Okay, this heart of darkness was not a dangerous, crocodile-infested, jungle-shrouded waterway in a failed state, but a shallow, twisty tidal creek with stagnant water that ran through the grasslands of the peaceful Sonoma Valley wine country.

Merrydale took a final deep breath and relaxed until Orr interrupted his reverie. He was yelling from the lower survivor's cabin.

"Commander, we have a little problem."

"Yes, Orr. What do we have?"

"A stowaway, sir."

The Commander whipped around. Mayor Hope Stinger smiled sweetly at him. She was standing on the steps that led down to the compartment behind and below the bridge.

"Hello, Commander. Thought you could use a little help."

Merrydale was stunned. He thought they had said a firm goodbye when he broke off the Coast Guard station tour.

"What the fuck are you doing, Stinger?"

"Helping out. Didn't want to miss the fun."

"I can't have you here."

"Well, I am here and, think about it, you may need my skills."

"As I told you back at the station, tonight's mission is military and it might get nasty. There should not be untrained civilians on board."

"You only have a crew of three. I know you'll need four."

"This is a military boat. We may have a firefight."

"That's okay. I'm in the Coast Guard Auxiliary. I've done the Guard's pursue and boarding training at Station Cape Disappointment in Ilwaco. I'm quite capable of being part of the crew."

"No. There's no way." The Commander pounded on the console in front of him. "Why? Why are you doing this to me?"

"Come on. I'm only trying to help."

"Right. I suppose you think you can handle a Sig?"

"I'm a qualified expert with the Sig at the range. Hair trigger. Boom. Boom. Boom. Nice, tight shot group"

"I still can't. I just can't. You'll have to stay below

when we board the boat we are chasing."

"What are we after here?"

"The two who broke into the yard and made off with a part of the SUBROC torpedo. And they have a hostage. This is on my watch, and I'm pursuing them."

"So how do you know who pulled this off?"

"Your usually dumbass Assistant Harbormaster Mitch. The marina CCTV video picked up the thieves carrying the stolen collar. You can watch them take it onto a boat in this marina and then motor off. The civilian trawler they boatjacked belongs to someone named Carver Pardon, who was clearly at the helm."

"And you think they came here?"

"Mitch again. He put his startup company's GPS target on the suspect's boat. We know where the trawler went and that it tied up an hour ago up the creek from here."

"Well, this sounds exciting. I'm itching for a fight. Aye aye, Commander. I'm looking forward to doing this."

"You'll have to remain below in that cabin."

"But then I'm out of the action. No, let me help with the fight. Please. I can do it, Commander. I can fight fiercely."

"Stinger. No can do. Stay below or regulations demand that I put you in restraints."

"Okay. Okay. I'll stay here. You know, I kind of like the idea of restraints. We can explore that after karaoke sometime."

The Commander didn't have time for her jokes. Or her alluring Dahlia Desire perfume. Or the sight of her in her white sailor suit dress. He would be breaking every regulation by continuing the pursuit with a civilian on board. But what could he do? The wily Stinger had outfoxed him.

It wasn't the first time. She usually prevailed during their beer-fueled weekly karaoke sessions at Padre Jaime's bar, tricking him into singing the Righteous Brothers *Unchained Melody* over and over. Then, in that magical afternoon tryst hours before she was to meet up with Hunter Callahan, the business-like Mayor had doused the romantic moment by unloading non-stop about her anxieties.

Still, regulations were clear—he had to keep her out of action. This ultimatum made him crazy. Once again, his uptight Coast Guard attitude was going to dink his social life. Buttoned-up Coastie military life didn't jibe with the give-and-take of infatuation. Now, how was she going to react to his unflinching rigidity with regulations?

Merrydale gathered the other crew in the bridge, explaining his attack plan. "Body armor mandatory. Upriver should take twenty minutes. We'll stop short and then dash in on my signal. Orr will be my wingman for the boarding. We'll position ourselves on the bow. Nelson stays inside to secure the boat, then follows." The Commander raised his voice. "Our stowaway stays in the survivors cabin."

He checked each of the Kevlar vests and handed

out Sig Sauer automatics to the crew. "We might have a hostage situation. So no firefight unless lives in danger. I sincerely hope we don't need them."

Hope's voice came from below. "My vest is not so very flattering. Compromises a polydactyl girl's figure."

The Commander's tone was grim. "The vest is absolutely vital."

"You're right, of course. Commander. Thank you again for this orientation."

"I'll have to deal with your presence later. However, you'll get to see what the Guard's assets can do in the prevention of international crime."

He turned to Nelson. "Start upriver slowly—five knots."

Nelson refolded the charts. "Aye aye. Captain. No problem. We should be riding a flood tide. Should give us at least two hours of confidence on this squirrely creek. We'll have plenty of depth to get to the old steamer stop of Wingo."

Nelson brought the pair of Detroit diesels to life, ran up the red handled throttles and backed off the anchor, then set a course north and rumbled into the mouth of Sonoma Creek. Merrydale and Orr moved to positions outside the bridge on the bow. The shoreline slipped by silently. Not even a ripple broke the mirror surface calm. The night was eerily quiet.

The Commander relayed his orders. "Keep us on dead center. I believe the channel is straightforward, at least up to Wingo."

"Aye. Aye," replied Nelson.

The diesels idled slowly through the shadowy fields of sawgrass stretching out to either side. They crept past a vineyard on the western shore.

"Nelson, where exactly are we headed?" yelled Hope from below.

"Wingo, your Honor. We're going to the Wingo Wharf."

"Oh, I know Wingo. That's just a couple of old deserted buildings."

"It is, but that's where we think we will find the stolen SUBROC collar. It's in a civilian trawler. And there's a hostage. So, be careful with any weapons. The hostage is the boat's owner, I believe."

In a quarter of an hour, MLB 88666 slowed at the last curve before Wingo.

"All stop."

"All stop," Nelson repeated

The Commander and Orr lay prone on the bow. It was now almost dark. Through his night vision scope, Merrydale could see Wingo's two deserted warehouse buildings on the western bank of the creek. A forty-foot trawler was moored next to the wharf at one of the buildings.

"Remember, watch out for the Sig's trigger safeties," whispered the Commander. "We are approaching the dock full tilt. Surprise gives us the upper hand for boarding. Everyone ready. Check your sidearms."

"Nelson, on my signal, bring it full. Make an s-curve toward the wharf so we approach from behind the trawler and our heading is upriver."

"Roger that."

Merrydale scanned the stolen boat a last time. It looked quiet. Only one light was burning in an aft cabin.

He rose to his knees out on the deck and yelled, "Now. Hit it. All ahead."

The diesels boomed to life and the bow rose as MLB 88666 accelerated across the turning basin for the last hundred yards toward the trawler. The lack of activity on the suspect's boat confirmed they had achieved surprise. They were closing quickly on the trawler's stern as Nelson began the tactical wide s-turn. Twenty yards from the trawler, its diesels roaring, the Coast Guard boat jolted to a stop. MLB 88666 had struck a submerged shoal and had run aground.

The lurching boat sent Commander Merrydale tumbling backwards, smacking his head against the superstructure, knocking him unconscious. His relaxed body rolled forward, slipped under the railing and plunged off the deck into the shallow water. At the same time, his sidearm Sig discharged, and the bullet struck his little toe on his right boot.

Orr managed to hold on through the shock, but Hope, outside on the port walkway, lost her grip and catapulted head first through the air, her arms spread out in a cross, weightless in the darkness until she splashed face down in the brackish water along the muddy creek bank.

Inside, Nelson quickly unbuckled his seat harness and rushed to the fore deck to help Orr lift the unconscious and injured Commander back onto the boat. They dragged him inside the enclosed bridge and Nelson began to remove his boot and treat the wound.

Orr went back up on deck and peered into the darkness. He used the powerful searchlight to hunt down Hope's white dress face down in the muck. She was stirring, though, and appeared to be trying to stand.

The Commander's gunshot brought the trawler's diesels to life with a roar. The suspect's boat accelerated around the front of MLB 88666, turned south and sped into the darkness. They were getting away down Sonoma Creek.

No one on the Coast Guard vessel had any opportunity to use a weapon. Except Mayor Stinger. She rose from the grassland along the shore and blindly fired four shots at the fleeing suspects before Orr yelled, "cease fire". The trawler had disappeared around the bend. Everyone on 88666 could hear them laughing.

The crew carried the unconscious Commander down to the survivor's compartment. Orr then went back on deck to rescue the Mayor. He jumped from the side walkway back into the muck and waded up to his thighs to reach Hope. She was woozy and was trying to find her Sig she had dropped in the briny water. Orr helped drag her the last twenty feet to the boat, before Nelson pulled both into the survivor's compartment. She stunk like rancid garbage but was awake.

"I'd have hit those escapees if you hadn't blinded me with that stupid light."

"I was only trying to find you."

"Well, you made me miss."

"Maybe we are far better off that you did," Orr said. He offered her soap and water and towels to clean up a little. "I can make java."

"I'd love some." She was shaking.

The semi-conscious Commander had been belted into the seat beside her but had slumped to the floor, landing with his face at her feet. He kept mumbling something that sounded like "poly-dack-till." Orr shot a questioning look at the Mayor.

Hope shrugged "He is really way out of it." She helped Orr pull him back into a sitting position.

Nelson returned to the bridge and began a quick damage survey. There was no leakage or fire. The bilges, the engine compartment, the auxiliary compartments, and the forepeak void were dry. He returned to the bridge and radioed Station Vallejo that the suspects had fled and were heading south down Sonoma Creek. The radio operator answered that Mitch had alerted them to the situation and that they had dispatched a twenty-five foot outboard powered high-speed Defender class Response boat with a boarding crew of three. Pushed to a top speed of forty-five knots, it would reach the Sonoma Creek mouth at about the same time the slow moving trawler made it to the outflow and could escape into the vast San Pablo Bay.

Strapping himself into the pneumatic command chair, Nelson fired up the diesels and ran RPM checks on both engines. They were fine. He used the manual helm to check the rudders and propeller shafts and then maneuvered the joystick control on the armrest, initiating a noisy, lurching operation to unstick the stranded boat. Alternating forward and reverse thrust rocked the hull. Luck shined on Nelson. After several minutes of scraping noises echoing through the aluminum hull, Nelson managed to loosen their boat from the mud. He backed gingerly into the creek, checked the RPMs again, turned around and headed south.

The radio crackled with transmissions from Vallejo station's Response boat. They reported seeing aerial flares ahead near the mouth of Sonoma Creek. Two airburst flashes and then another two. There was also chatter from a civilian boat on the VHF channel 16. A Mitch Wellborn reported he had used the Vallejo Municipal Marina's Whaler utility boat to block the channel with bright searchlights and was firing flares in a standoff with the suspect's trawler. The Coast Guard Response crew roared past Wellborn, turned on their own searchlights and fired their M60 machine gun across the bow of the suspects' boat. Two men raised their hands in surrender. A boarding party took them into custody. The rescuers found Carver Pardon gagged with a male incontinence pad and wrapped in duct tape around his legs and arms. They released him but he appeared dazed and dispirited.

A Coast Guard crewman stayed with the Doublecross while the others took the suspects and the freed hostage aboard the Response. They also pulled alongside the Whaler and questioned Mitch about why he had done such a crazy stunt to blockade an armed trawler without any weapons other than a flare gun. They did thank him for alerting them to the situation before he took off for Sonoma Creek.

Nelson had been monitoring all the channels. He passed the news of the capture down to the survivor's cabin behind the bridge. "How's the Commander?"

Orr held up two fingers in front of the Commander's eyes. There was a vague response. "He seems to be better. The bullet shot off the edge of his boot but only grazed the toe. Still fuzzy but I think he's coming around."

"And the Mayor?"

Hope gave Orr a thumbs up.

"She appears to be conscious, in good spirits but slimy."

"Good, Nelson said. "Then I'm setting course back to Station Vallejo. It'll be slow because I have to run the engines in lower RPM as a precaution. But I hope the Commander comes to fully before we get there, so he can explain what the hell happened."

24

The Inglorious Mission Returns

Word of the gun battle at Wingo Wharf and the drama at the mouth of Sonoma Creek lit up the emergency band monitors of the Bay Area's media outlets. Assignment editors pulled crews from dull school board meetings and ordered them to stand by at Vallejo Marina's A dock for the arrival of the Response boat with the suspects and the hostage.

Savvy Coast Guard officers kept the prisoners apart from the scrum of photographers and hustled them into the station yard. A spokesperson appeared but gave a very routine statement, lauding the quick thinking of a civilian boat captain, noting that two suspects were in custody, expressing relief that the hostage was unharmed, and saying the SUBROC collar was back under guard. She said an official investigation would begin immediately. She ignored the yelled questions.

Next to pull in was the Vallejo Marina's utility Boston Whaler. Mitch, carrying Chipper, stepped off and approached the reporters. He told a dramatic story about hiding in the reeds at the mouth of

Sonoma Creek, then confronting the fleeing vessel to blockade it before firing red parachute flares at the trawler. He described Chipper's barking as menacing. This standoff, he said, allowed the arriving Coast Guard Response boat to step in and clean up the takeover.

"Were you scared?" Asked one reporter.

"Didn't have time to think about it. The whole situation just sort of happened."

Before the reporters could continue, MLB 88666 docked at the Coast Guard section of the pier. The reporters ran from Mitch and swarmed everyone coming ashore. The Commander was groggy, limping, still covered in mud, but he managed a wave to the reporters as the EMTs stretched him out on a gurney.

Hope strode off the boat eager to talk, stopping at a bank of microphones for her dramatic retelling of the disaster at Wingo.

"It was past sunset and was dark. When we roared up full tilt, the boat hit some mud and we so jolted to a stop. The Commander and Seaman Orr had been on the bow, in position to board the suspect's boat, but the shock of going aground knocked the Commander unconscious against the bridge and pitched him off the boat. I was in the doorway of the lower cabin and tumbled over the gunwales into the water. The crew jumped into action to save us, but the trawler used that opportunity to circle our bow and head south, making their getaway. I managed to rip off four shots at the fleeing thieves but they didn't return fire. Our crew then pulled both the injured Commander and myself into the lower survivors' cabin."

"What happened next?"

"In the darkness and confusion, the trawler got away. I want to personally thank our crew. Seaman Orr and Petty Officer Nelson quickly had the situation under control. Orr stayed below to tend to us while Nelson radioed for help. Then Nelson rocked the boat and backed us away from the shoal. We turned and headed south, but the civilian Whaler and the second Coast Guard boat had already intercepted the thieves, taken them into custody, freed the hostage, and recovered the stolen item. Missions like this show how it is so important for our Coast Guard to protect our shores. Thank you to our local military for all they are doing. Right now, I need a shower."

"What about the Commander, you know, the leader. Is he all right?"

"A bullet grazed his boot in the firefight but I think he'll be fine. Right now, he is still a bit hazy. Remember, he smacked his head and was knocked loopy when we went aground. Thankfully, we didn't need him for the things that happened later."

"So he was hit while exchanging hot lead with the suspects?"

"I'm not quite certain. We'll have to wait for the accident board."

A Coast Guard spokesman arrived and whispered to the Mayor. She said "Bye everyone", and walked to a waiting ambulance. The Commander was already inside and it took them both to the Sutter Solano Medical Center.

The next day the *Times Herald* editors jumped on the local angle. Mitch was portrayed in a heroic role. "Daring Vallejo Marina Worker Blockades Armament Thieves."

The subhead "Coast Guard Crew Takes Two into Custody. Hostage Freed and Stolen Torpedo Part Recovered."

Another subhead "Vallejo Mayor in Firefight."

"City employee Mitchell Wellborn and his dog Chipper risked everything last night to block the escape of thieves who allegedly kidnapped a Vallejo boat owner and allegedly stole part of the Coast Guard's mysterious armament discovery."

The confrontation at the mouth of Sonoma Creek happened shortly after dusk. Wellborn used a MINSY startup Findola Tabs GPS target system to find the suspects' trawler, which then was fleeing south down Sonoma Creek from Wingo Wharf. Wellborn and his dog confronted the suspects' trawler at the mouth of Sonoma Creek and used flares and powerful lights to blockade the waterway. During that standoff, a Coast Guard fast Defender boat arrived and fired an M60 machine gun across the suspect's bow. They took them into custody and freed the hostage, Carver Pardon, the boat's owner, who is a live-aboard resident of the Municipal Marina.

Officials listed his condition as good.

Another Coast Guard boat had earlier chased the *Doublecross* up Sonoma Creek to the deserted steamer port of Wingo. When they attempted to approach the stolen trawler, their boat ran aground. That boat's officer in charge, Lt. Commander Noah Merrydale, was knocked unconscious and ended up off the boat with a bullet wound in the foot.

Vallejo Mayor Hope Stinger, a Coast Guard Auxiliary crewmember, was also thrown from the boat. The Mayor apparently regained her footing and fired her weapon at the fleeing suspects.

Crewmembers on the stranded Coast Guard boat rescued the Commander and helped to pull the uninjured Mayor from the shallow mud.

Commander Merrydale is expected to fully recover.

25

The Wingo Wharf Examined

The Coast Guard panel investigating the grounding at Wingo Wharf was scheduled for two days later. Captain Ernest Hook had been chosen to preside over the accident inquiry at Station Vallejo. Hook had a reputation as an uptight, old school fossil that ranted about regulations and discipline, bullied his fellow accident panel members, and humiliated any officers and enlisted personnel involved.

Commander Merrydale called an old friend at Coast Guard Alameda. That source had talked to Hook the same morning. "Noah," he said, "you're a bit screwed. Hook told me he wanted to fast track this one. That he resented giving up his weekly round of golf to sit through hours of endless, droning testimony. 'Blah, blah, blah', were his exact words. You know he delights in pointing out sloppy incompetence by junior officers. Excuses cut no ice with him. Hook would be happy to just chuck the offending crew into the brig, bust them all a rank or rate and save the Coast Guard the cost of this stupid hearing."

"Not very encouraging."

"Yeah, but your second on the panel is Commander Wallace Wally, a veteran officer and one tough SOB. During his career, Wally posted a legendary record of offshore boardings and seizures of drug-running vessels. He's a good man. Appeal to the warrior in him and you've got an ally."

"And the third?"

"Chief Marine Machinery Technician Gloria Horns. She doesn't have rank on you so she can't vote on the findings. She's there to explore damage to the boat. Her presence may ignite tension. Hook doesn't think women belong in the Coast Guard, except behind a desk."

The hearing finally began at 10 am. Hull and engine specialists testified that MLB 88666 had grounded on soft Sonoma Creek mud but had come out of it without any damage. Chief Horns began to grill the witnesses, but had to back off when Hook restrained her. "That's enough. Don't beat a dead horse," he complained, "the boat is fine. Let's move on to the obvious incompetence section."

Lieutenant Commander Merrydale testified next. "Suddenly, we were faced with a brazen theft from Station Vallejo in broad daylight. And the vital attachment collar of the SUBROC in our maintenance shed was missing. We had to move quickly. GPS tracking revealed their escape route across San Pablo Bay. I gathered a volunteer crew, chose Motor Life Boat 88666 because it was fueled, and took chase. When we reached Sonoma Creek, we had to wait for a flood tide to ensure clearance to an old deserted steamer stop called Wingo Wharf. We crept upstream carefully, finally reaching a vantage point where we could see the suspect's boat. I ordered the high-speed assault but it was cut short due to the grounding. That's when I was knocked unconscious and thrown from the boat. And my service revolver discharged. Also, during the chase, I was shocked to learn there was a Coast Guard Auxiliary member on board. I ordered her to stay sequestered in the lower survivor's compartment. During the last moments of the chase, she chose to stand outside on the portside deck, from which she pitched into the muck when the craft ran aground. Because I had issued her a Kevlar vest and Sig Sauer sidearm as a precaution, she found herself in a dangerous position between our boat and the suspect's. When they roared away, she rose from the slime," he continued, "and like a true warrior, fired her service sidearm at the fleeing suspects."

Merrydale also praised the bravery of his enlisted crew, Nelson and Orr, commented on the first aid applied to his toe, and finished by outlining the updated security restrictions for the SUBROC collar at Vallejo's Coast Guard yard.

Hook took voluminous notes during Merrydale's narrative. Observers could see his eyes roll when the Commander described the crushing jolt as MLB 88666 grounded in the mud. Peering over his reading glasses with an obvious disdainful look, Hook adjourned the hearing for ten minutes. Everyone expected a bloodbath when they reconvened.

And they were right.

Hook went for the kill. "Commander Merrydale, do you believe that any officer who flouts regulations should be in command of a vessel?"

"I suppose that would be based on individual cases, sir."

Hook could be seen counting items on his yellow legal pad. "What if I told you that I believe that you, as officer in charge of this boat 88666, ignored at least fifteen regulations while recklessly taking a vessel in pursuit of criminals?"

"I'd have to say that conditions that day demanded that action. We are Coast Guard law enforcement, nautical warriors, not a bunch of namby-pamby rule-bookers who are afraid to pursue, board, and capture lawbreakers on the seas."

Hook's face reddened. "You mean putting yourself, your vessel and your so-called band of nautical warriors and, Lord help us, a female-type stowaway, that putting them in harm's way was a good idea?"

"Sir, we were chasing lawbreakers that violated the sanctity of our Coast Guard station. My crew had trained for the kind of danger we would encounter. The stowaway was tough enough to hold her own."

"Did you really believe that you could take a vessel that draws four and a half feet up a creek with a seven-foot clearance? And at night? And didn't you consider that this shallow watercourse might have muddy shoals or submerged objects?"

"I expected there would be clearance up to the Wingo Wharf."

"But did you check the charts for Wingo Wharf."

"Yes. Back at the creek mouth. After that, it was hot pursuit and free the hostage, so we had to act swiftly. My plan was to surprise, board, and takeover. We are fighters, not boat mechanics. In this case, we got stopped by a little mud."

"Commander," asked Hook, "you alone pursued armed criminals without bringing in backup. You led a crew into harm's way and used a bonehead strategy in the darkness. You shot yourself in the foot, went ass over tit off the vessel and knocked yourself out as it ran aground. Might you now look back and think this was a reckless command decision?"

"No, sir. And I object to the word bonehead. Surprise was our best option. I'd do it again. If we crept in, they could still hear our diesel and we would have put our boat in danger from possible automatic weapons fire?"

"But you had weapons?"

"Yes, I issued Sigs and the crew was wearing vests."

"So, you had one. Your Coxswain Nelson had one. Your Boatswain Orr had one. Am I to understand you gave one to this, this fetching stowaway?"

Chief Horns interrupted. "Sir, I must object to your constant description of the stowaway in sexist terminology."

"Well, Chief Horns, I'm only making an observation that God gave some women beauty. Both men and women can see that. You've got to admit it."

"Sir, that is a chauvinistic observation not worthy

of a senior officer in the Coast Guard."

"That is my opinion. You, Chief Horns, are a junior member of this board. So I remind you to watch the tone of your remarks. Let's move on."

Commander Merrydale hoped to settle down the agitated Captain. "Sir, the stowaway is in the Coast Guard Auxiliary. She had trained at station Cape Disappointment in boarding and live fire drills. And she qualified expert in range shooting with the Sig."

"And how do you know all this?"

"She told me."

"You accepted the word of a woman stowaway? What if she had lied?"

"I trust every member of the Coast Guard, male or female, if they have the training. For this operation, we needed armed fighters who qualified with the weapons. I watched her handle the Sig. She appeared to know her way around it."

"And that must be why, after apparently falling off the boat into the mud, this highly trained female auxiliary rose up to wildly fire four rounds into the darkness without your orders to do so. And then, she lost the weapon in the mud."

"She was in a tough spot, sir. She was trying to stop the fleeing trawler."

"And you didn't tell her to cease firing."

"At that point, I was unconscious, sir. My boatswain Orr yelled ceasefire."

Hook ran his fingers through his hair. He groaned in an overly theatrical manner. He threw his pen in

the wastebasket. "Commander, I just cannot understand how you can justify what you did. You were
reckless and impulsive and could have cost the Coast
Guard a million dollar piece of equipment and the
safety of yourself and your crew. And you did this
with a civilian woman aboard. I must say your lead-
ership that day baffles me."

Commander Wally came to life. "Captain, if I may,
I'd like to interject my thoughts."

"That's all I have. We've got enough solid evidence
for incompetence. But you may go ahead, Commander
Wally. Be quick."

"Commander Merrydale, I have listened to this
account. You were under pressure to correct a wrong
committed against the Coast Guard. You did respect
due diligence in waiting at the mouth of the estuary
for depth clearance. Your choice of a high-speed dash
to surprise and board the suspect vessel was a sound
tactical move. So you ran into a little mud. No damage to the MLB. No foul. And the toe injury was not
serious. This shit happens with live fire in combat. I
would, however, suggest that in the future, you organize backup before leaving the station. Or call for
it when you can. That's all I have to say."

Nelson testified next. He said that he feared the
Sonoma Creek estuary might be shallow in places
but that he had monitored the depth readouts and
tried to steer to the center. He was apprehensive
about the high-speed approach. "I guess it was our
only option that wouldn't leave us a sitting duck. I

tried to get as close as I could to the suspect's boat but it just wasn't meant to be."

Horns began to interrogate Nelson about his post-grounding survey of the boat's hull, props, rudders and diesels but Hook interrupted, shot her a stern look and told her to knock it off. "All that engineering mumbo-jumbo is irrelevant for the negligence finding that I'm sure will be coming."

Seaman Orr followed Nelson to the stand. He described the chaos when the boat slammed to a halt, and then his struggles to drag the unconscious Commander back onto the boat. He also told how, after he heard shots, he yelled cease fire into the darkness and then jumped into the estuary to pull the Mayor into the boat.

Mayor Stinger was next. She said that she had been on a civic orientation tour of Station Vallejo when the Commander and the crew were called to the mission. Yes, she testified, they asked her to leave the station. "But I didn't want to miss the excitement. It sounded like so, so, so military. And I thought it might be fun."

Hook groaned when she said "fun". He scowled and buried his face in his hands. "Mayor Stinger. A boarding party with a possible firefight is not fun. Stowing away on a Coast Guard boat is not fun. Firing lethal bullets from a Sig into the night is not fun. You put people in jeopardy because they had to consider your safety while completing the mission. You forced Boatswain's Mate Orr to jump into a dark, muddy marsh to pull a helpless thoughtless woman back to the boat. What if he had injured himself in that process? Your actions were inconsiderate and juvenile and demonstrated a glaring emotional weakness."

There was dead silence. The Mayor's face reddened. Chief Horns turned. "Sir, I am going to speak."

Hook waved his hand submissively. "No, just hold off for now."

"No, I am within my rights to make an entry into the record. Now."

"Go ahead. I can't shut you up anyhow."

"Sir, in case you haven't noticed, a goodly portion of the Coast Guard is female. We fly helicopters, captain cutters and act as district commandants. Women have been part of the Coat Guard for over a hundred and fifty years. I find your last derogatory insinuation about the so-called emotional weakness of the female gender to be not only uninformed, but actionable under the 2012 diversity guidelines and I am putting you on notice, yes I am, that I will report this to my commanders at Coast Guard Station Alameda."

Mayor Stinger jumped up from the witness chair. "Right on, sister. Right on. Sir, you are a sexist throwback. A Neanderthal. I too will report your attitude to the Commandant of the Coast Guard and possibly to the Joint Chiefs of Staff. You may not be aware that my father was an admiral in the Navy and that I have so many friends in high places. I know patriotic Republican journalists like Hunter Callahan of Fox

News. Keep this in mind—I'm just so, so getting started with you. Captain. If the findings of this hearing end up as negligence, or if there is any mention of that in the summation, your career, Captain, will be in my crosshairs. You'll be lucky to be captain of the bilge cleaners at a garbage scow dry dock in Iceland."

Chief Horns grinned. Commander Wally smiled. Hook reached down and put a sheaf of papers into his briefcase. "I think this hearing is over. You two females are free to do whatever you want. Right now, Mayor Stinger, your testimony is no longer needed nor appreciated. Get the hell out of here."

The Captain banged the gavel. "There will be no more witnesses. The panel will meet to discuss its findings. Everyone concerned will be notified in due time."

In an unusual move, the official Coast Guard accident board ruling was posted that afternoon. It found that the grounding was an artifact of the heat of battle and that all the crew had performed in proper manner. Nelson and Orr received commendations for their actions in the incident.

Commander Merrydale never heard another word about breaking fifteen regulations. The Commander received a commendation for daring to chase the thieves up Sonoma Creek, a medal for his wound, and a reprimand for not calling for backup before leaving Station Vallejo.

The transcript of the last minutes of the hearing, including the exchange between Hook, Horns and

Stinger, was somehow lost in an electronic hacking of the Coast Guard archives. It was blamed on the Russians.

Captain Hook requested and was granted early retirement. He relocated to Arizona.

Mayor Stinger was put on Coast Guard Auxiliary probation for her independent action firing a service pistol while trying to stop the fleeing suspects at Wingo Wharf. She also received a contradictory short letter from the Coast Guard Commandant commending her aggressive action to stop the fleeing suspects.

26

The Chicken Tamale

After resting for a day, the Mayor arrived back at city hall to find sheriff's deputies rounding up the last of twenty anti-pot-plant demonstrators. They had trashed her office for a third time. The air was hazy with the now familiar marijuana fumes. Papers were tossed about. Plastic water bottles filled the wastebasket. They had opened one of the thirty cardboard boxes stacked around the walls. And the office was now decorated with a dozen foot-high Jaylyn-a-Naut dolls.

Her assistant Lettie was tidying up, putting the dolls back in a box.

Hope held one in her hands. "So, when did these dolls get here? And why are these boxes stacked here? In my office?"

"The truck brought them last night. I had nowhere else to put them for the moment," Lettie said. "These are the Chinese ones. Is this what you expected?"

The mayor turned it over. It was a soft rubber copy of the Mermaid Queen complete with a tiara and a fish tail. But it had a surprise feature. It was very generous anatomically. The coconuts barely covered the doll's enormous breasts.

Hope looked disappointed. "This is not quite what I was thinking about. It is obviously Jaylyn's face, and her African-American skin color, but in person she's a skinny one and this doll makes her way too chesty. Don't you think?"

"Yes. And watch." Lettie pulled the arms back into a vee shape behind the doll so it looked like it was flying. The mouth opened a little, and the doll made puffy moans as its eyes became dreamy. "I don't know if everyone will like this."

The mayor tried it on the doll she was holding. "Omigod. How would you interpret that particular face?"

"In ecstasy. Dreamy."

"Dreamy. Could she be dreamy from the excitement of flying?"

Lettie laughed. "No, Madame Mayor. That's wishful thinking on your part. This look is pure bliss, if I've ever seen it. Orgasmic afterglow. Rapture."

"So, pull back the arms and our Jaylyn-a-Naut has a happy ending?"

"That's what I'm saying."

"Do you think this'll be trouble? I mean when we hand these out?"

"Yes, Madame Mayor. Huge breasts. Ecstatic reverie. Big legal trouble might be coming our way." Lettie put the last doll into its box and returned to her office.

Hope sat down to ponder this.

There was a knock. "May we come in?"

The Mayor looked up to see Lettie return along with three others from the office staff. Lettie was carrying a lone chocolate cupcake with a single candle.

"Sure." Hope said.

They burst into song. "Happy birthday to you. Happy birthday to you. Happy birthday Madame Mayor, Happy birthday to you."

Hope gave them a smile. "Thank you. That's so kind of you."

"So, what is it this year? I count thirty-five," Lettie said.

"That's right. Moving right along."

"Suppose you've got a big night planned?"

"No, just a quiet time at home. But thank you again. This means a lot to me." The trio chatted and then left. The Mayor found a birthday card in her in-box. It was from Mitch and Chipper and had a dog's paw print on the envelope.

Birthdays had never mattered. But this one, well, it was a life marker. And tonight, she would indeed be alone. The Commander was on duty, and there was no one else—no friends or family to celebrate with.

Hope's attention drifted. Few knew that the city's go-ahead mayor, who attacked every issue with bluster, had started to agonize over personal milestones. This unease had been growing. She was getting to an age for breeding. And she'd have to take this in hand.

She had bet the farm on the Commander and his military bearing, and had ignored other offers. The last temptation had been a fantasy hookup with Bald Chad of the Lowlife Squats. But that ended after the debacle at the Frog Pond Java Hut when she demanded to sing.

Hope phoned the Commander. Of course he was at work. Of course he was busy. But yes, he would join her for dinner tonight at the little Mexican place in nearby Benicia. And, he said, he had a surprise for her.

Hope arrived first, finding a place on the banquette along the wall. The Commander strolled in ten minutes late and dropped into the chair opposite her. "Hi, Hope. Anything good here? I'm really hungry."

Hope was in a quandary. The Commander's clothes were neatly pressed and he smelled like after-shave. She watched him ceremoniously take off his jacket, fold it with care and place it on the seat cushion beside her. At that point, a switch in her brain clicked off. That's when she knew this was a come-to-Jesus moment. She was on the verge of a decision. That night.

Hope tried to smile. Of course he really didn't know it was her birthday. She had never told him. Now the thirty-five milestone had been reached and the long-range picture needed attention. But this man across from her was a question mark. Yes, they had an afternoon of satisfying sex. Still, no doubt he ironed his underwear. She knew in her heart that she didn't want a brood of little Commanders.

Tonight would be a watershed. The future loomed. Until any family unit she produced got off to a solid start, she would need a partner with available hours to help. And there was the trial of waking up every morning facing the same partner in the sack. She would like someone tall. Over six feet. And buff. And rugged. And funny. This guy at her table was short in a number of those areas.

The waiter appeared. Hope ordered the molé burrito. The Commander asked for one taco and a diet cola.

There was her family history. In her youth, her mother had been an adventurer, traveling alone around much of the world, working for NGOs in community development projects in South America, getting arrested and jailed in Thailand, and spending a year assisting a war journalist covering dusty trouble spots in the Mid-East. Then, out of the blue, she had hooked up with the stiff, uptight Navy officer who became her father. Her mother, she thought, had opted for a stable personality with routine to deal with the brood of children. Later, when she and her two sisters fled the nest, it spiraled into an alcoholic haze until her parents split up.

The waiter reappeared with her burrito plate and a chicken tamale for Noah.

"That's not what I ordered," he said with a grim tone. "Take it back."

The waiter looked at her note pad. "Uh. It says here a chicken tamale." She showed the order to Noah. "See."

He was infuriated. "No chicken tamale. A carne asada taco. I ordered a carne asada taco. Write that down. Now get that…"

"I'm sorry…"

"And you can get the manager too."

Hope turned to the teenage waitress. "No, honey. Forget the manager. Just get him his taco." Then she turned to Noah. "Hey, take it easy. It's just a slight mistake."

He was yelling. "No. It's incompetence. She's got to learn discipline."

That was it. The decision was done. Whatever hesitation she had, well, it dissolved. No use wasting time on candidates who were not tenable. "You were pretty fucking rude," she said. "That ruins tonight's dinner for me."

"These people have to get it straight. Take responsibility."

"Look. She's a high school kid. Give her a break."

"No, she's got to come around. Achieve the highest standards."

"Noah, don't be such a tight ass."

"I'm only asking for proper table service."

"I guess this is as good a time as ever to talk."

"About what?"

"It's time we figured out where we are going?"

He looked a bit miffed. "I thought things were sailing along. And I have to tell you something that I realized today."

"Which is?"

"I know your secret. I remember it from when you lost your shoes and I was delirious after Wingo Wharf. That's why you demanded we leave the lights off when we were making love that afternoon."

Hope sat back. "What are you talking about?"

"You are polydactyl. Polydactyl."

"So what. I have an extra toe. Big deal. It makes me a better hunter."

"But no one else knows. It'll be our secret. Especially after this next part."

There was silence. Hope didn't know what has coming.

"I'm getting transferred. To Ilwaco, Washington. To Cape Disappointment."

"When's that going to happen?"

"Pretty soon. I was hoping you might think of coming with me. You know I lost part of one of my toes and you have all those extra ones, Miss Polydactyl."

"To Cape Disappointment?"

"Yes."

"I've been to Cape Disappointment. There's a reason it has that name. No one ever thought it should be Cape Delightful. My answer is no."

"No. But we are perfect for each other. And I love you."

She blurted out. "Today's my birthday. I'm thirty-five. Only my assistant and Mitch my doggie co-parent gave me cards. You didn't, but then I never told you. You might know about my physical oddity, but there's a lot you don't know. Look. Although we sing great karaoke together, Noah, you are not the song for my future. And I don't want you to get the wrong idea thinking that our relationship is really going forward. It's not. We've run aground."

"Wow. Where's all this coming from? I guess I should say happy birthday?"

"Yeah, but that's a moot point. This conversation now is about my future."

"I thought it would be our future. We are in love."

"No. That idea has sailed."

Noah was silent for a long time. He smacked his fist on the table, upsetting the salsa dish. The waitress reappeared with the reheated chicken tamale. "Here, you can have it. Your taco will be here soon."

"I told you, I don't want the frigging chicken tamale." Noah swept the plate off the table and onto the floor. Part of the salsa spattered on the waitress, who broke into tears. The other diners looked over.

Noah stood. "So, does any of this have to do with my command attitude at Wingo Wharf? Are you disappointed because I shot myself in the foot? Did that figure into you reasoning?"

"This has nothing to do with Wingo Wharf."

"Be honest, Hope. Were you mortified that you got a slap on the wrist but I got a medal for taking a round?"

"Nope. And, of course, you got a medal for shooting yourself."

"Then, what is it, Hope? You want to throw away our love. Our future. Should I tell everyone that you're all show and no go?"

"You really want to know?"

"I deserve to know."

"You're too stiff, Noah. You are just too damn stiff for my needs."

❖

27

The Doll Disaster

"City to Sell Lifelike Flying Mermaid Doll"

It didn't take the *Times-Herald* editors long to sensationalize their exclusive. The anti-pot protestors had stolen one of the Jaylyn-a-Naut dolls and given it to the paper. The front-page story featured a side-by-side photo comparison of the real life Jaylyn Chadwick flying through the air set against the Chinese knock-off doll promoted by the mayor.

Both had their arms spread out backwards.

Both had dreamy looks.

But only one had enormous breasts.

Jaylyn was furious. She was quoted in the article. "This ugly invasion of privacy makes fun of me. My attorney has already filed for an injunction to prevent the mayor and the city from distributing this travesty."

The story estimated that the city had four hundred dolls. The mayor's office would not comment.

This edition sold out quickly. National web news services picked up the story and labeled it as trending on many news feeds. The item became a worldwide sensation in the weird news genre. It made the inside first section page of the *New York Times* and was fodder for daylong blather that drives the cable news channels. Fox News' Callahan Cabal spent a half-hour rehashing the details.

Mitch loved the story and was gloating until he turned the page and found the Coast Guard Wingo Wharf accident board findings that absolved nearly everyone of responsibility.

He went ballistic. Chipper cowered in the dog bed watching an angry Mitch storm around the marina office, kicking furniture and banging his fists on the metal filing cabinets.

Mitch screamed. "They ran aground. Two of the crew fell into the mud. The suspects escaped. Two sidearms were fired. An idiot officer shot himself. Himself. How could there be no responsibility? Accident my ass."

In Mitch's view, everyone, except Mitch, did almost everything wrong.

Still, this story was only a trigger. His principal worry—he was going broke. Marketing consultants pushing his two-person MINSY startup, Findola Tabs GPS, had drained his personal bank accounts with their fees. Product design, packaging, paying Ukrainian coders, and inventory costs were steep. Sales reps were having trouble getting marina owners to cough up the bucks to try out the system, and they reported that this was the wrong time of year for industry investment.

The dollar squeeze was going to force Mitch to find a little on the side. He restarted his water taxi charter service for extra income. Promotional cards advertising his personal thirty-two-foot cruiser now sat beside cash registers at most local tourist stops and convenience stores. That's when a surprise walked through the door.

It was Carver Pardon, looking tired but using a cane.

"Professor Carver, glad to see you on your feet."

"Thanks. I'm still a bit stiff after being tied up for so long."

"I hope you'll be back teaching the Wednesday espionage class. I think what you've been telling us is fascinating."

"What part really hits you?" Carver asked. "In a visceral way?"

"The business about spying on your own people. Like the Navy here. About running the Buckhorn dance hall on Georgia Street just to listen in on the sailors. And, of course, about ghost agents where the agency has replaced dead ones with new identities."

"Well, that stuff went on. And still does." Carver picked up the *Times-Herald*. "So, what did you think of the Coast Guard findings on the Wingo Wharf debacle?"

Mitch shrugged. "Thought it was the usual bullshit covering one's behind."

"What did you expect? Reality?"

"I guess that's sort of utopian. Right?"

"So, who are those suspects they arrested? The Coast Guard redacted their names," Carver said. "But

I'd like to find that out."

Mitch smiled. "I heard scuttlebutt that those guys were hired agents who operate out of Marseille. That they were in contact with an agent here."

"If you get names, let me know."

"Will do, professor. So, what's happening today? You know I almost killed myself the other day while we were looking for you."

"So I heard."

"Everyone wants to find out about the Trap Door group. But I think I fell through it. I had this epiphany, laying there on the cement floor, that your buddy Valerie Beckett wasn't looking for you at all."

"She's not my buddy, pal. In fact, we are at war. In our business, you don't make friends. And don't believe everything that dotty old woman tells you."

"So what can I do this morning for our noted right-wing blogger."

Carver handed him the water taxi business card he picked up at the *Sardine Can*'s cash register. "I need to find a captain and boat for a short local charter."

"Your boat or mine? It's three hundred for me for the day and a hundred fifty for the boat. Or four hundred for a half day. Where were you thinking of going?"

"Your boat to Wingo Wharf."

"So, back there. Why not just take the *Doublecross*?"

"The Gestapo has put my trawler under house arrest for the time being. They say it's evidence. I can live in it, but not move it an inch." Carter looked tired. "I'll take your half-day option. Can we leave in the morning?"

"Yeah, if I can if I get someone to watch the worm shop. Shouldn't be a problem."

Four hundred.

Mitch needed the dough.

As the sun rose, Mitch hadn't seen any sign of Carver. He wandered down the dock to the *Doublecross*, jumped to the aft deck and knocked on the cabin door.

There was no answer.

Mitch pushed the door open. Carver was on the floor of the cabin, writhing and mumbling. His body shook and a crust of white foam encircled his mouth. Mitch stepped outside and called 9-1-1.

The EMTs arrived in minutes and hauled Carver off to the Sutter Solano Medical Center. Mitch was left behind in the cabin of the *Doublecross*. After calling Maggie, he innocently pawed through some papers on the settee table. These had hand made drawings of the SUBROC torpedo missile and its parts, showing the attachment collar along with notations on the side. He folded that up and put it in his parka pocket.

Now Mitch didn't know where to turn. Maybe it would be Maggie.

28

Carver's Battle at the Hospital

Doctors at the Sutter Solano Medical Center Trauma Unit gathered in the hallway, admitting they were baffled. A newly admitted patient, Carver Pardon, had arrived in the ER confused and with trouble breathing. They suspected a mild stroke or seizure while aboard his boat. But neurovascular tests discounted these diagnoses. Routine antibiotics did nothing. Meanwhile, the seventy-five-year-old ex-agent lay semi-conscious in the ICU, his eyes often glassy and non-responsive. There were suspicions that a mysterious internal virus was festering, and if it reached his heart or brain, the prognosis would not be good.

Carver's only known family was his brother, George, in D.C. During his lucid moments, hospital social workers convinced Carver to sign an Advanced Health Care Directive naming his brother as the primary agent. If Carver was unconscious, George would make the call. Valerie got them to list her as the backup.

The hospital staff gave Carver special status, allowing Valerie and Maggie to visit despite not being immediate family. On the second afternoon, while the pair sat in a nearby waiting room, a familiar face appeared with a bouquet of flowers. Maggie was shocked. It was Krista, the older community worker from the U.N. squalor project in Serenity Point.

"Krista. I'm surprised to see you here?"

"I heard Mister Pardon was sick. I came to cheer him up with these flowers."

"Where did you hear he was sick?" Valerie asked.

"I don't remember. It must have been at the marina."

"From Mitch?"

"Yes. From Mitch, I think," Krista answered.

"Where did you meet Carver?" Valerie was angry. "Where? Tell me where?"

"Up at Serenity Point. He was out there one day."

"In his boat?"

"No, I think he drove. He was looking around. Promise and Jaylyn weren't there. We had a long talk."

"You are a liar," Valerie said. "Maggie, call security. Better safe than sorry. I don't think this woman should be allowed anywhere near Carver."

"I should be allowed. You see, he was my father. That's what he told me. He dated my mother while working at the navy shipyard forty years ago but then he left town before she knew she was pregnant. She ran away to Canada where I was born. Then she went to Iceland, where I was brought up."

"A likely story." Valerie stood nose to nose with Krista.

"Did you work for the U.N.? Really, or was that a cover?"

"I did work for them. And it's true that he is my father. I had tests. Check it out, whoever you are. He knew details."

"No, I just can't believe that story."

Two hospital guards appeared in a minute. Valerie showed them her agent credentials and confessed her suspicions. The guards hustled Krista away.

Maggie was confused. "That's very interesting. Carver her father? Why would he tell her that? We should check that out."

"No, leave it. Forget she was here. Security will take care of it."

"What are you so jumpy for?" Maggie asked.

"Remember when I told you there was only a single mention of the Krista in the summary of the UN project."

"Yeah."

"Well, it just doesn't make sense that she would appear in a sleazy place like the Delta. I think she is an agent."

"So you suspect the Icelanders were after something?" Maggie asked.

"Not all of them. Not the younger ones. Only Krista."

Valerie and Maggie walked down to Carver's room. He was looking old and weak. Intravenous lines ran into both arms and an oxygen tube was clipped to his nose. Screens on the wall displayed graphs of heart rate and blood pressure. He struggled to smile.

"Hi Carve," Valerie whispered.

His voice was raspy. "Speak up."

Valerie raised her voice. "I said hi. Looks like they are taking care of you."

"Say again?"

Valerie looked at his ear. "Oh. No hearing aid. You're an old man and your hearing is gone. Have them put the bloody things in your ears."

"Mmm." Carver signaled the nurse, who moved the oxygen tubes. "Any information on my prognosis?"

"Carver. Haven't talked to the internal meds doc right now," Valerie said. "But when you arrived, the admitting staff told us they think you have raging internal infections."

"What does that mean?"

"I don't know. This is all vague. But your old body has to step up and fight them."

Carver's voice got weaker. "Please bring me something to read? Nothing to do here."

"I can bring you an audiobook. You can listen," Valerie said.

"I'd like that. A mystery. Le Carre. Any of his old ones. Or a thriller?"

"Yes, of course. More espionage. The same old Carver."

Carver reached out and pulled Valerie's arm so her face came closer to his. "I'm worried that this is it."

"No, not for the time being. Concentrate on getting

out of here and getting healthy again and back to your boat."

Carver coughed. His focus wandered. He struggled and thrashed. "What...what if I don't?"

"You will. Maggie and I are here to help you pull through."

More coughing. "No, this is unbearable. Let me tell you, Val. You should look carefully at Wingo. Everything else, you'll find everything you need on the *Doublecross*."

"Find what?" Asked Maggie. She edged closer to Carver before he grabbed her wrist.

"All of it. Including my will. You'll be surprised. Then, find Erika. Promise's mother. In Todos Santos. In Baja. She knows all the gossip," whispered Carver.

"Knows what?" Maggie asked in a barely audible voice.

Carver squeezed harder on Maggie's wrist. He tried to swallow but could only make rasping sounds through his throat. His hands flailed in the air. There was fright in his eyes. He was in a rough patch.

Valerie stuck her head out the door into the open medical station. "Someone" she yelled. "Quick."

A nurse ran to the room. She hit the emergency button that called for a crash cart and a doctor. Then she pushed Valerie and Maggie out, suggesting they wait in the family areas.

Valerie checked with hospital security. They interviewed Krista and couldn't find anything out of place. They let her go.

Twenty minutes later, a social worker came and

said that Carver had slipped into an unconscious state. Maggie banged her hands against the soda vending machine. "I shouldn't ever go to hospitals. I don't know what to say to people in pain. I didn't know what to say to Carver."

"It's okay, Maggie. Nobody ever does," said Valerie.

The pair waited another three hours bathed in the flat fluorescent glare of the visitors' lounge, but there were no developments. So, they finally left.

At six the following morning, the hospital texed Valerie.

Carver Pardon had died during the night. Peacefully, in his sleep.

Valerie called Maggie and then drove to the marina. The two women hugged each other and sobbed. Valerie also put in a call to his brother George in D.C. He wasn't shocked by the news but asked her to schedule a cremation and arrange to have the ashes shipped back east. She agreed to do that.

After that conversation, Valerie realized there was no one else to tell. He had no friends as far as she knew. And very few in the modern intel community would be sad that Carver was gone. Just another older ex-spy at the end of the road.

The next night, Valerie, Mitch, Maggie and Chipper gathered in the cabin of the *Angry Duck*. Valerie brought a few bottles of Templeton's Rye, Carver's favorite drink. The somber group began to do shots, toasting Carver's life or what they knew of it. Valerie told some shocking anecdotes of his years as a field agent infiltrating right-wing nationalist groups nearly a half-century in the past.

They finished off two fifths of Templeton. Everyone was pretty drunk. Valerie announced there was more to be done. "You know, I think I'm ready now to follow his last request. Tomorrow, we have to search the *Doublecross*." Valerie looked to Maggie. "But now we've got work to do. And it will be heart wrenching. We've got to sift through Carver's things."

"I guess we do," Maggie said. "You know, I've been thinking about what we don't know about Carver. What if Krista really is his daughter? What did he mean when he said Erika will know? I still don't know what he was getting at."

"I think there's lots to find. Let's get started."

"What's the hurry," protested Maggie. "It'll have to be in the morning. I'm too drunk now to concentrate."

"Get plenty of sleep. We may find out a lot." Valerie said.

29

The *Doublecross*

At dawn, Valerie showed up for coffee at the *Sardine Can*. Her eyes were red and her always-perfect makeup was caked-on and uneven. "Crying all night," she admitted. "Losing Carver was tough. God I wish he had taken better care of himself. It's more than just losing an old colleague. This is an omen. He was my generation of spies, and now I am on the sidelines and watching the older ones die off, one by one."

Maggie looked unkempt too, having binged on the wine and Templeton's rye last night. "Sorry you have to go through this. You know, I did like him a lot, but I almost hated him at the same time."

"Yes. I guess his recent return to action in the search for this missing warhead was too much for him. But he was still a factor. He could muddy the waters. And when my old bosses guessed he was orchestrating things, well, that brought me west. Now, that mission has been interrupted." Valerie sighed. "I guess it's time to go down to the *Doublecross* and see if we can find his papers."

"Whatever," Maggie said.

The pair finished the food in silence and paid up. The *Doublecross* was moored out on B dock. Although the police had seized the key to the aft cabin, Mitch had a spare set and let them in.

Inside, it was messy. Papers were scattered on the counter tops and the floor. Piles of clothes were set against the bulkhead. "It looks like someone else has beaten us to it. Hope they didn't find any of what we are looking for."

Maggie thought it creepy to rifle through a dead person's belongings. She half-expected his ghost would burst through the door and scream at her for disturbing his things.

They began at the two-drawer filing cabinet. Valerie felt underneath the drawers and retrieved a manila envelope that had been taped to the bottom. "Well look here. Looks like our predecessors missed something big."

She held up a pile of old photos. Maggie peered over her shoulder. Young men in white uniforms. New ensigns. "Graduation from Annapolis," Valerie said.

A group shot on the dock beside the sail of an attack sub. "I guess this must be one of his duty tours."

There were six or seven photos of Carver in civilian clothes, drinking in various bars with crew cut men.

"More male officers," Valerie said. "No pictures of girlfriends on his motorcycles. Not much of a romantic soul, is he?"

Maggie disagreed, saying he was quite handsome as a young officer. Inside an old cigar box, Maggie found two medals and several collar insignias. All were dull and clouded with grime. "Don't think he wore these on Veterans Day," she said.

Valerie extracted another envelope. Inside was Carver's will.

"Omigod. Look at this. It says he is leaving this boat, the *Doublecross*, to Promise Pazty, whom he calls his daughter, and to his other children, whom he doesn't name, as joint heirs."

Maggie sat down. "Is that what it says? Promise is his daughter?"

"Written right here. If she predeceases him, and no other children come forth, he wants the boat to be sold and the money goes to, ready for this, you."

"I thought Promise was my father's daughter. Except, of course, by another mom."

"Doesn't look like it. Carver should know."

"This is going to be an atomic shock for Promise. I mean, for forty-five years, she thought this handsome, cavalier French officer who could be still alive somewhere was her father."

"So, she may not be your half-sister any more?"

"That would be another conclusion." Maggie felt dizzy. She sat on the forward bunk and put her face in her hands. "This is a helluva find."

"Should we go on? Or do you want to stop for today."

"No, let's look some more."

Valerie turned up another envelope with black and white photos of what looked like a family standing on the porch of a substantial clapboard house. There was snow on the background. "I think this is his brother George. The two children could be his nephews." Valerie said.

Another photo showed a skinny Carver with three women and a second man, a dark-haired thin officer with a mustache and wearing a foreign uniform. Maggie grabbed it. "Oh my god. This is a picture of, I think, my father. With my mother, Promise's mother and I believe that is Teresa Almeda. And, of course, Carver."

"So, we can assume he knew everyone back then," Valerie said.

"It sure looks like it. But why would he? This one looks like he was close to everyone in this photo."

"Why would Carver be hanging out with this group?"

"Don't know. Surely not meditation? He wasn't really in their circle."

"Do you think this picture was taken anywhere around here?"

Maggie scanned the photo. "There is a wooden building in the background. You know, if I could guess, it looks like it could be the wharf warehouse in Wingo. Carver wanted to hire Mitch to go back there. Before he died."

"Maggie, we need to make a trip."

"To?"

"To Wingo Wharf."

"Okay, you head to Wingo. If I can find someone to go with me, I'll make a lightning fast trip to Baja. Maybe with some luck, I can dig up Erika, Promise's mother."

30

Baja's Revelation

One bad experience twenty years ago while travelling alone on a desolate Mexican highway made Maggie fearful. This time she needed a companion, so she turned to Mitch. He could speak a little Spanish and had ridden motorcycles in the Mexican desert in the Baja 500 races.

"Hell, yes, I'll go. I'll get Hope to take Chipper. I'm ready right now."

"You know it's not all fun and games. We're hunting for someone."

"I'm okay with that. Just indulge me for some street food and I'm fine."

There was an airfare bargain on an Internet travel site for an immediate trip. The next afternoon they were stepping into the piercing sunlight at the San Jose del Cabo airport. A banged up white Toyota Corolla waited at AutoRentz. Mitch insisted they stop for street tacos in San Jose. As they headed up the western coast, Mitch made Maggie park a second time so he could bodysurf in the roiling Pacific Ocean. She put up with that. An hour later, they arrived in the sleepy artist and surfing enclave of Todos Santos,

on the Pacific Ocean forty miles north of Cabo San
Lucas.

Carver had mentioned Todos Santos at the hospital. Promise thought this might be where her mother
Erika may have ended up. Once in town, Mitch
bugged passersby and store clerks, hoping for clues
to an ex-pat named Erika. The woman behind the
counter at the El Tecolote Bookstore pointed them
down a dirt road to the west. Two blocks from town
they found a hand-painted sign saying "Serenity Sur"
next to a driveway. Maggie parked under the canopy
of a healthy mimosa tree. Its fragrant blossoms perfumed the air.

A thin older woman wearing a wide straw hat was
digging with a shovel in an outdoor vegetable garden.
Her skin was deeply tanned and wrinkled.

"Erika" Maggie asked.

"Who wants to know?"

"Erika, it's me, Maggie Trout. Sally's daughter."

Erika walked up to Maggie. She stared at her.

"Yes, I am Sally's daughter."

"Go away," Erika said.

"No, it's time to talk. I have news of Serenity."

Erika softened and gave Maggie a hug. "So, you
are Maggie. I thought you had that look. Who's your
friend? Not a federal agent, I hope."

"Just a guy I know who likes to travel around
Mexico. Mitch. This is Erika."

Mitch reached out and shook her hand. "Mucho
gusto," he said.

"Mucho gusto," she replied.

"Well, wow. You are here. Why? And how long can you stay?"

"We have tickets back for tomorrow."

"My god. You came all this way for only one day. I've been here for more than thirty years. This is a magical place."

"Wish we could stay longer. But we have to get back to Serenity."

"Well, I have spare bunks here." She eyed Mitch, who had unbuttoned his short-sleeved cotton shirt. "Do you need one or two rooms?"

"Two." Maggie said. She shrugged but with a tiny smile.

Erika invited the visitors to her casita, a compact, two-room single story whitewashed box with a red tile roof. They sat under a larger mimosa tree around a table made from an old industrial cable spool. Erika went inside and returned with icy fresh orange juice. She told them her story.

She had been a South African weapons scientist of mixed race who immigrated to the United States in the 1960s to escape apartheid. At MINSY, she said she became disillusioned with the weapons program and fell in with idealistic dissident scientists. They were hounded by the government until she fled, finally hiding in a fishing camp on the Sea of Cortez for ten years. U.S. DEA agents, looking for stolen hallucinogenic drugs, discovered her. But because the chemical stimulants she had taken were legally hers and because the American government had not yet criminalized them, the DEA couldn't file charges against her. They let her stay lost in Baja.

Maggie unloaded her news. "The military found a missile in the Mare Island Strait and since then, there's been a frantic search looking for the missing nosecone. One investigation had been run by someone we think you knew, Carver Pardon, and the other by an East Coast agent, Valerie."

Erika gripped her wrist. "Carver always told us to beware of Navy investigators. This Valerie might be the one. He said they used retired freelance agents called ghosts. They worked for powerful people high in the Navy brass, operated with a free hand and were very dangerous. Nearly fifty years ago, he had battled with one particular woman, a contemporary of his, and joked about her slender body, short hair and big ears. I don't remember her name."

"Omigod. That sounds like Valerie. I wondered about her," Maggie said. "That's about her age and description."

"The last time I spoke to Carver, just before he left for D.C., he was still wary of this woman. Probably over forty years ago. But it does indeed sound like her," Erika said.

"Promise needs to know this. I'd better call her."

"You won't get a signal out of here. You have to call from the highway on the other side of the mountains."

Maggie put her phone away. "Okay, later then, and sorry to tell you this but Carver died just last week."

"That's sad. But the last time we spoke was so long, long ago."

"So, I'm curious. Who was the leader of your group?"

"We didn't have a leader. That was the era of communal decisions. We would get together up at Serenity and have endless discussions about what to do next."

"Were you the one they called Major Tom?"

"Like I said, group decisions. It wasn't a top down organization."

"What did you guys hope to accomplish?"

"To build a weapon that would inebriate a region for a short time. Yes, make a whole city goofy. To be a demonstration of the power of these terribly destructive bombs. We thought it was a critical idea at the time. Better than thermonuclear. But there were many complex drawbacks with our theory and we hadn't thought it through."

"How did you keep this a secret?"

"It was easy. Carver was part of the Navy's criminal investigation unit that was looking for us. And he was in our group. So I had to trust him even though I never knew whether to trust him. Then he went back to D.C. and we never talked again."

"So when did you panic?"

"Carver sent a coded message that the Navy was getting close. So we all decided to flee. Without telling him, we dumped most of our SUBROC in the Napa River. The attachment collar we left in a secret workshop in some old coal tunnels under the ball field.

We took our experimental anti-warhead in the nosecone to a hideout at an upcreek backwater called Wingo Wharf."

"It's there. Omigod, both Carver and now Valerie discovered that place."

"Well, let them search all they want. After Carver and René left, your mother and Theresa helped me move it. We hid it away in the Delta."

"You mean at Serenity?"

"Yeah, if you really want to know, and it's probably still there. I hope no one will ever find it. But if they do, then our legacy might go to the wrong people. It's old tech but reactionary groups could use it. You need to keep them from getting to the bunker."

"The bunker?"

"It's my old art studio. In the levee. Only Promise knows where it is. And once you can warn her, she knows what to do."

Maggie handed Erika a packet of snapshots of Serenity Point. These old black and white candid photos brought tears to her eyes. "We were so young. And look at Carver. He just looks passionate. He was quite the man. A very complex man. An idealist, and a horny snake. I mean, this was the time of free love and he made screwing the government and screwing every woman who worked at MINSY his goal. I never was sure if he was into his ideology or just sex. It was good sex too. At one point, I thought I loved him. But that turned to ashes. I'll tell you a secret. He was Promise's father."

"We guessed that from his will. He said she was

his daughter. And we think he might have had another daughter. Named Krista. She showed up saying
she was Carver's daughter."

"Very easily could have been. He never let his
pecker rest. Krista would be Theresa Almeda's daughter. Theresa got pregnant and moved to Canada and
then to Iceland, where I guess she married."

"Omigod," said Maggie.

"And," Erika shrugged, then looked at Maggie, "sit
down for this. Carver was probably your father too."

There was dead silence. Maggie cleared her throat.
"Excuse me? My father was the French Lieutenant."

"No, it was Carver. But your mom never told
Carver."

"You mean my mom never confronted him. And
she lied to me for all those years. All those years."

"Listen, Carver lived a life of lies. He had this
line—that he had suffered an injury while on submarines and therefore was shooting blanks during
lovemaking. His sperm, he said, was benign. Wrong.
Your mom and he had a very brief fling. Very brief.
She chose to keep everything a secret because of
Carver's Navy commission. And I'm sure he would
have wanted her to have an abortion. He tried to get
me to do that too. Not the family type. So your mom
Sally went to live with a relative in the Gold Country
while she had little you. Carver was already back to
Washington. They listed the French officer René as
your daddy, but he was gone too. Sally told me it was
Carver. And until she married your stepfather, she
brought you up all alone."

Maggie wept and spoke in a whisper. "So that liar," she said, "that bastard, he was my real father."

Erika was very matter of fact. "So you find out a bit too late. I'm sorry dear, but that's the truth. Now you know."

"And after that?"

"We got the hell out. Carver was in Washington. René already went to southern France. I went to Laguna Beach in California before coming here. That's where I had Promise. Then I went back to Serenity and stayed under the radar. Your mom married the deputy sheriff and raised you. Teresa took off for Canada."

Erika, Maggie, and Mitch spent the rest of the evening drinking Pacifico beers and going over old times. In the morning, they took Erika's suggestion, and headed back to the airport on a short cut across the peninsula, a road east from Pescadero through the Sierra de la Laguna. One kilometer shy of the east side highway, a late model sedan passed them, and then turned to block their path. Two men got out of the car with automatic pistols.

"Uh-oh," Maggie said.

Mitch and Maggie handed over the their wallets and phones. The larger of the two thugs then shot out the tires of the rented Corolla.

"It's one kilometer to highway one. Enjoy the walk, Gringos."

The men drove off.

The winter sun was bright but the temperature only about seventy degrees. When they reached the highway, an old rancher gave them a ride to the San Jose del Cabo airport. Their plane had left. The car rental company had already been alerted to the abandoned sedan. The police took copious notes about their story and referred them to a Mexican tourism group that distributes temporary aid in extreme cases. They arranged for a room at the El Encanto in San Jose Del Cabo, offered a free shuttle ride there and back, and handed over coupons for food. The airline booked them on a flight the next day.

Maggie and Mitch checked into their motel. A couple from France allowed Maggie to use a cell phone and call Promise. There was no answer but she left a voicemail. "Delayed a day for return. Be very careful of Valerie. Might be a ghost agent. If anyone gets to the art studio, Erika says you know what to do."

The tourist coupons got them a free dinner and a drink. Afterwards, under a starlit sky, they sat out by the tiny courtyard pool, laughing about the path that led to this place.

By ten, both were exhausted. Maggie slipped her hand into his while they returned to the room. Inside, there was only one very uncomfortable queen bed with a hard mattress.

"Awkward, eh?" Maggie said with a smile.

"To say the least."

"I guess we are sharing this one."

"If that's okay with you," Mitch said.

"To be truthful, Mitch, I've been so busy trying to scratch out a freelancer's living with the camera.

What I mean is, I've just been working and haven't been intimate with anyone for maybe three years. Also, had a rotten experience when my ex escaped with that teenage aromatherapist child. Kinda turned off my urges for this sort of thing."

"You know, we don't have to do anything. Just sleep."

"No, I'm game to see what happens."

Mitch started to take off his shirt, exposing a large anchor tattoo on his shoulder and an inked Samoan design encircling his arm.

Maggie touched the ring near his elbow. "Nice tats. But you go to the gym and I don't, so let's keep the lights off."

Mitch flipped the switch. In the dark, both finished undressing. Even with the window air conditioner rattling noisily on high, and a ceiling fan roaring at top speed, it was too hot and humid to use a blanket. Maggie showered first. Mitch followed and by the time he finished, Maggie lay naked beneath a sheet.

She faced the wall, and sobbed. "Sorry. It's all about Carver. No one told me the truth for forty-five years. All of them. Including that bastard Carver. Apparently my father."

Mitch slipped gingerly under the sheet and put his hand on her shoulder. "So sorry, Mags. I guess it's going to take a long sad time to process this. I am always ready to listen. If that'll help."

Maggie turned to him. She wiped her tears on the pillowcase and spoke in a low voice. "Thanks. I'll have to get over it. It is what it is." She paused. "You know, it's surprising to hear you call me Mags. I used to hate that—I mean you using Mags. But now I don't mind it. It seems very natural." She sobbed again. "This might work out. I mean we might."

Both rolled over and faced the wall. Then Maggie giggled and snuggled up against Mitch. When Mitch turned to put his arms around Maggie, she relaxed and let him. The next moments were clumsy. And clammy. The humid Mexican night made intimacy the enemy of desire. Along with Maggie's occasional hot flashes, the heat was insufferable. They kicked off the sheet, both lying naked in the dark.

Finally, sleep came. Sometime just before dawn, Maggie had a rotten dream. She cried out and thrashed and then sat up. Mitch slept soundly beside her. She whispered to Mitch. "You know, I know we're good for each other."

And she wrapped her arms around him.

31

The Ghost Agent Unmasked

About the same moment Maggie and Mitch were boarding their return flight in Cabo, Valerie pulled into the dirt lot at Serenity and parked between two wrecked runabout boats on rusty trailers behind the Shipwreck Café. Following instructions, she honked three times. Promise emerged from the *Henry David*, threaded her way across the rotten docks, climbed over the levee, walked to roadside and stuck out her hand to Valerie. "Hi. I'm Promise. Welcome to Serenity."

Valerie shook it. "Thanks. Maggie here yet?"

"She was due to fly back yesterday. I expected to hear from her. I'm sorry about your co-worker Carver's death. I read all about the battle at Sonoma Creek and how they rescued him. Sounded quite exciting. Too bad he didn't make it."

"Thanks. Carver was pretty weak when the kidnapping started. He never took care of himself. He had diabetes and heart problems. Then the thieves must have tied him up for days. It really took the life out of him."

"Come on. Let's go back over the levee to the boat. Jaylyn is still here. But she will leave soon for the new semester of classes."

Both tiptoed across the rotten boards on the floating dock, careful to step over the missing ones. At the *Henry David*, they jumped to the deck and went below to the cabin.

Jaylyn introduced herself and all three sat down at the foldout table. Promise poured her a coffee. "Is it decaf?" Valerie asked.

"No, but I have some. Do you want the decaf?"

"Yes. Doctor's orders. Just can't process the caffeine anymore."

Promise ground a new batch of beans and filled the coffee maker.

Finally, Valerie spoke up. "Promise, there's a lot to cover. But first, some unsettling news. During the search of Carver's boat, after he passed, I uncovered critical personal information you should know. Don't hold it against me. This may cause you to rethink your history."

"I don't understand," Promise said.

"Your father might not have been a French naval officer, but rather someone who lived in Vallejo." Valerie reached into her case and pulled out a copy of Carver's will. She had taken the original to a Vallejo attorney with whom she had contracted to handle the estate.

Promise scanned the document, reading each paragraph in a deliberate fashion.

"This person, the same one who was kidnapped, Carver Pardon, is leaving me his boat? And also to Maggie?"

"That's right."

"Because he thinks I am his daughter?"

"That's right."

"But I don't believe it. I've never heard of this guy. My mother never said anything about anyone else."

"Possibly she wanted this information to stay below the surface. I think there were many dangers of admitting he was the father."

"Where has this guy been for forty-five years? Why didn't he speak up? Could he just be bullshitting everyone?"

"No, I think your mother must have felt it was easier to keep up the lie." Valerie handed Promise a copy of the group photo.

"Omigod. That's my mom. Then there's René, who I thought was my dad. And there's this other guy."

Valerie smiled. "The other guy is Carver."

"Omigod. When?"

"Before you were born. Sometime around 1970 we think," Valerie said. "There's also Maggie's mom Sally and another friend named Theresa Almeda. Everyone worked at the shipyard."

"They all are so young."

Valerie paused for a moment. "Do you know where this photo was taken? We thought it was Wingo. I took a boat there yesterday but couldn't find any angle that would replicate this."

"That's no wonder. That's not Wingo Wharf. That building in this picture is the back side of the retreat building here, now the Shipwreck Café."

"So, these people had gathered here at one time."

"I would suspect many times. A lot of people came to the retreat center and my mom's art studio. This was a busy place while the Navy ran the shipyard."

"This art studio. Is it in the building with the Shipwreck?"

"No. It's a ways from here and built into the levee."

"First let's go to the Shipwreck. I'm trying to wrap everything up, so it might be worth doing it," Valerie said as she stood.

Promise wondered what was the rush. But they left the boat and followed the path over the levee and across the dirt parking area to the Shipwreck's deck. Then, Promise stopped for a moment. "You guys go on. I've got to check my voicemail."

Valerie and Jaylyn walked to the outdoor deck of the Shipwreck. There were two old tables built atop wooden spools.

Promise finished checking messages.

Valerie pointed to the tables. "How long have you had these? Big industrial spools that used to hold electrical cables, right?"

"I think a couple of our local light-fingered residents swiped those from the utility district years ago. They finished the tops nicely. But they've been here for as long as I remember."

"And the base of each table is?" Valerie asked.

"Old shipyard leftovers. We were told the bases

were from fixtures used on submarines," Promise said.

Valerie stepped onto the deck and tapped on each base. Both sounded hollow.

"These are from a submarine. These are torpedo nosecones."

"Uh oh."

"And my guess they are from SUBROCS. Underwater guided missiles."

"But they've been here around forty years."

"Exactamah. Don't know what is inside, but you may have been eating lunch on a five-kiloton thermonuclear warhead."

"Eww," Jaylyn said.

"No, I know these are hollow. I mean, I've seen them when we moved the tables. We tilted them on their sides," Promise said.

"So, where did you get these cone bases?"

"They were stored in my mom's art studio," Promise answered. "In the levee bunker."

"And how far is the bunker?"

"It's about a quarter mile along the channel."

"Do you go there often?"

"No, it's filled with junk. And old metalworking machines my mom used for her welding art. It was her studio."

"It might be very important we go see this now. What's inside could be dangerous." Valerie said.

Promise warned about the ticks and snakes. "Jaylyn and I will have to get some long pants," Promise said. They returned to the boat. Promise told Jaylyn about Maggie's message.

"What will we do?" Jaylyn asked.

"I don't know. Play along for the time being, I guess."

Ten minutes later, the group set out along the path. The thermometer had risen into the nineties and the trio was pushing through waist high weeds. At the bunker, they shoved aside the decaying powerboat that camouflaged the entrance. Promise sprayed some lubricant on the locks, and then opened the pair of security doors. She fired up the generator and flipped on the lights.

Jaylyn and Valerie followed her inside. A moldy stench was overpowering. Faded photos of three women, the French officer and Carver Pardon, all working in the bunker were push-pinned to the corkboard on the wall. Papers and blueprints were scattered around on various worktables.

Valerie discovered a mockup SUBROC attachment collar and nose cone atop a wooden shelf against the back wall. "I need help. This one," she said, "must weigh two hundred pounds." Jaylyn and Promise joined her to move it to the worktable. It was jammed with an elaborate spider web of pipes and tubes.

Valerie spent ten minutes examining the nose cone and taking smartphone pictures of the inner workings. "We'll need to get some of my specialists into here. Don't touch anything else. There are explosive detonators lying around and they are so old, they might be unstable. Let's lock up the workshop."

Promise was unsure of what to do. "So, what did you find? Is this it? Is this what everyone was looking for?" She pointed to the cone on the table.

"Yes. At last. And it is very valuable," Valerie said.

Jaylyn was shocked. "Then let's get out of here. If this stuff is so dangerous."

Valerie answered. "She's right, Promise. Anyone within a half-mile might be in danger if this is volatile. I'll get the Navy to check out everything here and then take it away to be disarmed. You know, this nose cone was not your mother's property. It belonged to the Navy. In fact, why don't all of you go back to the Shipwreck and I'll be along."

Promise frowned. "There is something weird going on. Valerie, you aren't just curious about the nose cone, are you? I'm not really sure who you are working for?"

"No, I'm working for the government. It doesn't matter which part. My job was to find this nose cone and keep Carver from getting to it first. Keep him from selling it to the highest bidder arms dealer. But finding it here makes me wonder if he knew where it was all along. He was old and failing but I think his brain still worked. He was leading us all in circles. He got us to that red herring Wingo Wharf. But now we have the Mollusk in our hands. The genie is out. You two should leave right now. It is not safe in here."

Promise put both hands on the nose cone. "Jaylyn give me a hand. Let's turn it over." Jaylyn joined her and they grunted and shoved the nose cone toward the edge of the workbench.

Valerie stood firm. "Hey, what are you doing?" But the nose cone's momentum forced Valerie backwards. She stumbled onto the floor on her back. Promise continued to push the Mollusk. It fell off the table, landing on Valerie's calf and left foot. There was a loud crack as her leg bone snapped.

She screamed. "Aiiii. Why'd you two do that? I think you broke my leg. God it hurts. Get this thing off me."

"We'll do that." Promise was not sorry. "I'm not going to let you, whoever you are, just steal my nose cone. So we'll have to get help for your leg. Or maybe, we'll carry you back to the Shipwreck." Promise went through Valerie's pockets and took out her cellphone and her automatic pistol.

Jaylyn found a piece of wood and after they shoved the nose cone off of Valerie, she aligned the stick with the fractured leg and wrapped some duct tape around it for a splint. Valerie sobbed and breathed in short, puffy huffs. "You two. You don't know what trouble you are getting yourselves into."

The two women hoisted Valerie to waist level and carted her outside. Then they began half-carrying and half-dragging her along the path back to the Shipwreck. Each time her leg banged against the ground, she screamed. When they were close to the Shipwreck they stopped. Promise used a rock to smash Valerie's cellphone before throwing it into the slough.

"That was so fucking stupid. That had the pictures

on it." She kept screaming. "God it hurts. My leg is broken. Wait until I report this. You all will go to jail."

"We'll take our chances."

"Look. Ow. Fuck. My leg hurts. We can make a deal. Go back and close it up for the moment. I'll see that specialists examine what's inside. And we'll forget about this little incident."

"Just stay quiet. We'll have you to the Shipwreck in no time. But first I have something to do. I'm going to close it up."

Promise walked back toward the bunker. In ten minutes, she returned along the path, running and breathing hard. "Everyone hunker down. It's gonna blow."

Valerie frowned. "What have you done?"

"Sorry but you're not going to get to touch it again. I did get a message about ghost agents. You must be one of them. My mother gave me strict orders that if anyone suggested taking this stuff away, no matter who they were, that I should just blow it up. So, I set off the self-destructive explosives scenario."

"But why? The Mollusk warhead might have great benefit for its scientists."

The ground shook as a thunderous explosion rocked the levee. Chunks of earth and cement flew into the sky and rained down on the women and surrounding brush.

"Omigod," Jaylyn said, brushing aside a coating of dirt. "It really blew."

"That's outrageous," Valerie said.

"Yum," Jaylyn said. She had a rapturous smile. "I

felt that one with a peculiar joy."

Back at the Shipwreck, Valerie continued raging about sending the pair to jail. She told them not to call 9-1-1. Instead, Jaylyn called a number Valerie gave her. In an hour, a car pulled up with two muscular men with shaved heads. They were the ones from the *Sardine Can.* They pointed automatic weapons at Promise and Jaylyn

Valerie had calmed down a bit by now. "Ladies, I am going to my own medics right now to set my leg. So, we don't want you two to do anything rash. That's why my friends here will tie you up and gag you. My guess is that someone will find out in a day or two. By that time, we'll be gone."

The gunmen took both women to the *Henry David* and wrapped them up in duct tape. They left each on a bunk in the darkened cabin.

"Sweet dreams," said Valerie.

The next day, there had been no messages from Promise. Maggie and Mitch drove to Serenity and Maggie poked her head down into the *Henry David.* "Promise? Jaylyn?"

She saw the two trussed in the duct tape. Using a scissors, she freed them.

"Valerie. Valerie was the agent. I had to blow up the bunker."

Maggie sat down. "Erika warned us but it took a while to get a signal out. Anyhow, I suppose by now, they have disappeared. Gone to ground somewhere."

"Probably."

"And there's no longer a serenity warhead?"

"That's right," said Promise. "Serenity's warhead has gone kerblooey."

32

The Pre-Re-Sail Gala

There was a knock at the stall door. "Madame Mayor, can I come in?"

"Go away, Lettie."

"No. Let me in. I saw that nasty process server hand you the envelope as you waltzed in the front entrance."

The Mayor unlocked the door. Lettie crowded in.

Hope had been hiding in the women's restroom stall, steadying herself for the trouble to come. Outside, in the Front Room restaurant, closed for tonight's city sponsored Pre-Re-Sail Festival bash, two hundred city workers, a throng of A-list political celebs, and numerous free-loading news crews were drinking free wine and gobbling cheap cheese on the city's nickel.

"So what was the important notice?" Lettie asked.

"Oh, some silly court order about the dolls."

"Exactly how silly?"

"An injunction forbidding us to distribute or sell any of the four hundred anatomically exaggerated Jaylyn Flying Mermaid dolls in the United States."

"Was that all?"

"Not exactly. It says we have to get rid of them. Tell me, Lettie, tell me how I can explain to my blood-thirsty political enemies that we are going to destroy the little buggers? This will drain the city coffers of over forty thousand dollars."

"I have an answer." Lettie beamed. "My church is in contact with an orphanage in Balkhash, Kazakhstan. They have been pleading for toys for the kids. We send the dolls there, and claim that Vallejo is seeking to become a sister city to Balkhash. Neat, eh?"

"Do I know anything about this Balkhash?"

"No need. It's very modern but remote. And no one knows anything about it. Besides, we can have as many sister city arrangements as we want."

"Okay. Sounds like you've saved my ass again."

"My job, Madame Mayor."

"Anything else I should do?"

"Yes, if you get any questions about the dolls, pivot and highlight our exciting news—that a startup techie company on the MINSY grounds has gone golden."

"You mean the deal with that Seattle-based tech Lastex buying up MINSY startup Findola Tabs GPS is actually going through."

"Yeah, for twenty million. And, your Chipper's co-parent Mitch is going to clean up."

"How wonderful for him," the Mayor said sarcastically.

Hope left the stall, touched up her makeup and emerged into the crowd. Partygoers stood in clusters balancing drinks and snacks in their hands. The chatter from conversations was deafening.

As the news of the startup buyout spread, Mitch was surrounded. Hope headed for him, threading her way through the hubbub until someone grabbed her hand. She turned. It was Garrett from the Lowlife Squats, with a silly grin on his face.

"You've been gone so long. I thought you fell in."

"Yeah. Old joke but hi," she said. "What are you doing here?"

"I came to help my old man set up. He's pissed at you for that night at the coffee shop."

"That was my fault. I just had a few wines and was in the wrong mood. But stay with me now, please."

That's when Maggie yelled for everyone to shut up. The noise levels rose louder. Holding a mic, she climbed onto a table and again demanded silence. This time it worked. "I'm raising my third glass of rosé," she yelled in a commanding voice. "Another toast to our newest mega millionaire. Mitch. He's the only super rich guy most of us will ever know. When he moves away to a mansion somewhere, the worms in the bait shop will miss him. To Mitch."

The crowd cheered and responded "To Mitch."

Mitch smiled. Chipper was at his feet, beaming. Mitch climbed up on the table and Maggie handed him the mic. "Thank you Mags. I'm not rich yet. There will be moolah, but it's going to be in stock that will be untouchable for quite some time. So, until then, I'll still be driving the rusty pickup, still be Assistant Harbormaster, and still be selling worms, eating hot dogs and chips from the bait shop. Now, on a more serious note, I'd like to invite the Mayor to join us for a few seconds of silence to remember a Marina resident, a former Navy officer on our attack submarines, and an American patriot who passed away recently. He served our country in many ways. Everyone, please raise your glasses to the memory of Carver Pardon."

Garrett helped Hope climb onto the tabletop.

Everyone quieted down. Then a voice yelled, "Pardon was a traitor."

Mitch turned to see Lieutenant Commander Noah Merrydale in his Coast Guard dress uniform. His face was red with rage and he was slurring his words. "Turncoat. He shold our counstry down a river."

"Maybe you should keep quiet, Noah?" Mitch demanded. "I think you're out of line and a little drunk."

"I just know it. Yup. I know it. Pardon was a frigging disgrace. He served two masters."

Noah jumped up on the table next to Mitch and stood inches from his nose. He shot his hands toward Mitch's neck as if to strangle him. The Mayor stepped between them. At that point, the Commander grabbed Mitch's shirt and the table legs folded, giving way and sending Maggie, the Mayor, Mitch and the Commander crashing to the floor.

No one was hurt but Mitch was livid. He reared

back to smack the Commander but thought better. Instead, he released him and yelled, "Go home. Noah. Get sober."

The Commander threw his shoulders back, smoothed off his coat, did a smart about-face and walked unsteadily to the exit. He noticed Garrett standing comforting Hope. "Sonny boy, watch out for that Mayor. She'll lead you on to think it's love. Then, she'll discard you. She's all show and no go."

Hope said "Noah, you are fried to the gills. Why don't you give someone your keys and we'll call a cab for you."

The Commander waited for some time, looked intently at her and said, "To think I actually had fallen in love with you." And Noah executed another military about-face and strode quickly to the exit.

Hope whispered to Garrett. "I hope he's all right. Why don't you go out and see if you can talk him into a taxi."

"Sure," Garrett said.

While the crowd reset the collapsed table, the Mayor asked for quiet. Chipper ran over, sat at her feet and gazed up.

"Hello, everyone," Hope said, putting her hand on Mitch's shoulder. "Well, that little dustup is over. And as the mayor of this tough as nails town, I would be remiss not to celebrate our local startup's generosity. Mitch Wellborn, after only one day of being a MINSY techie zillionaire, has now volunteered that, when the windfall money comes in, he'll kick in a quarter of a million dollars to the Solano County Food Bank. Let's hear it for someone putting his wallet to work for the community."

There were cheers.

"Recognizing this, I would like to proclaim a bogus resolution from the city." She pulled a stick of gum from her purse and acted as if she was reading it. "It says…'To Mitch, the city council can only say whereas, whereas, and whereas.' That's it, I guess. Thank you for thinking of your community."

The Mayor gave Mitch a hug while Chipper beamed from the floor. Nothing makes a dog happier than to see his parents stop bickering and make up.

Maggie refilled her wine glass a fourth time with rosé and pulled Mitch aside. She had tears in her eyes. "That was touching. I mean, about Carver. I want to thank you."

"Only sorry that you didn't know the truth while he was alive."

"Can't help that. Lying and deception was his life. Not mine, though. Just wanted to say how happy I am that we have found each other." She gave him a kiss. "And if you abandon me now that you are a rich bastard, I'll track you down to the corners of the world and put hot needles under your fingernails."

"Won't happen. You'll just have to save those hot needles for someone else."

By this time, the Lowlife Squats had set up a small bandstand in the corner. Chad nodded his head, and they began their new hit track, *Fly on My Own*, the insipid country ballad celebrating the story of Jaylyn Chadwick's near death blastoff.

When they finished, the Mayor asked for quiet again. "I know that you might get tired of hearing *Fly on My Own* tonight, but it is a big old nation-wide country hit. Our Vallejo Brand is getting an enormous boost out of this one. You should know that I have donated every cent of my co-writing royalties from this number one song to the coffers of Vallejo. As for tomorrow, we'll see the exciting Re-Sail Fest. Combined with Waterfest, these nautical efforts have been kind to the city. We have sold two million dollars worth of swag, including posters with Jaylyn's face, toy submarine models of El Gordo, and tour shirts for the Lowlife Squats next summer. We have even donated dolls of the flying mermaid to a children's orphanage in our sister city of Balkhash in Kazakhstan. The statue of Jaylyn, just outside on the shoreline walk by the telescope, is a monstrous hit. Ten thousand selfies were taken there in the first week. Now, enjoy the rest of the party, because tomorrow we'll have the resurrected yacht parade, thirteen food booths selling the scrumptious American fish sticks, a wonderfully inventive kids bouncy house, and Jaylyn Chadwick's return to Vallejo to recreate her adventure on the Mermaid's Flight ride."

The crowd whooped and applauded. Garrett reappeared beside her. "He took the taxi. He was really blotto."

Hope smiled at him. "Garrett. Remember I asked you if you go to karaoke bars?"

"Yeah. But I don't."

"But I do. How about this Friday night. After the Fest. See you at nine at Padre Jaime's karaoke session. I can really do the Righteous Brothers. "

"The bar by the freeway. I'll try. But I don't know the group."

"They are from way back. But soulful." And she started to sing…"Oh, my love, my darling, I've hungered for your touch…."

The next day's Vallejo police blotter recorded the arrest of one Lieutenant Commander Noah Merrydale outside Padre Jaime's karaoke bar at 2:30. He was charged with being drunk in public and causing a public nuisance by refusing to stop screaming the words of the Righteous Brothers song *Unchained Melody* "Are you still mine. I need your love, I need your love" over and over, while holding his shoe as a microphone.

He was released in the morning and all charges were dropped.

33

The Re-Sail Fest Ride into the Sky

A two-story high inflatable balloon replica of El Gordo, the drug-smuggling mini-sub, guarded the front gate for Vallejo's Re-Sail Fest. This bulbous creation doubled as a kiddie bouncy house. Once inside, fairgoers could wander the huge shoreline lawn dotted with booths. These offered the chance to buy a working El Gordo model, a Mermaid's Flight poster with Jaylyn's rapturous face, a hoppy IPA from the Mare Island Brewing Company, or they could get a greasy sample from one of thirteen competing fish stick food booths.

On the cultural side, the music lineup featured high school jazz combos, local dive bar country bands and Vallejo rappers.

Many families came early, eager to see the yacht parade aborted four weeks ago when El Gordo blew up in the channel. The weather had cooperated initially—the sky a bright cerulean blue with puffy white clouds ringing the horizon. But a worrisome stream of suspicious smoke had begun leaking out from BigWeed's nearby shoreline marijuana processing plant, spreading a light psychotropic mist across the festival grounds.

To the north near the Causeway Bridge, the decorated boats awaited the parade's start. The impressive Coast Guard Motor Life Boat 88666 Golden Gate was festooned with streamers and would lead. Hope, dressed in her iconic white sailor dress, blue Vallejo Yacht Club blazer, and Cleopatra-like gold laurel wreath headband, had taken a place on the prow of the lead vessel, her shoulders back and chin out, ready to wave to adoring voters along the shore.

Only two news teams made any effort to cover this. The others had taken a pass, refusing to pay the license fee now needed to report in Vallejo.

At exactly ten, the yachts moved out amid a cacophony of air horns, and jockeyed to form the single line-of-march. Visibility was declining over the Mare Island Strait, as more pot-laced smoke billowed from the troubled factory and spread in waves across the festival grounds. By the time the slow-moving lead Coast Guard boat reached the judges, the spectators were restless. Then, a mystery craft cut into the line in the second slot. It was Carver Pardon's Hatteras 42 Trawler. The Mayor's assistant, Lettie Melendez, texted the Mayor. "An uninvited bogey in second position. Do you want me to have a security boat run them off?"

"No," the Mayor re-texted. "Leave them be. Let it ride."

From its topmast and rigging, the crew unfurled a huge banner. "To honor a cadre of rebellious pacifist scientists and workers who tried to redefine the equation of nuclear standoff during the Cold War, please remember MINSY workers Teresa Almeda, Lt. René Guilbot, Erika Pazty, Carver Pardon and Sally Trout."

The crowd in the bleachers, now mildly stoned from the second hand haze, gave the serious banner a wild response.

The Mayor texted Lettie "I'm choking out here. What gives with BigWeed's factory? Is it on fire?"

Lettie replied. "Yes. Roaring blaze in bud warehouse. Columns of smoke spewing out. Haze very funky here. Everyone weird. Think all slightly crunked."

Once passed the bleachers, the Coast Guard's lead craft circled back and tied up at the dock next to the ferry terminal. The Mayor stepped ashore, finding it hard to contain her giggles as she greeted the VIP guests. A small crowd gathered and she steadied herself in front of a bank of microphones.

"Good morning, Vallejo. Is everyone having a goooooood time?"

The crowd was giddy. They screamed "Yeah".

"There's so much to do here today. I mean, be sure to stick around for the Squats band at two. That Chad is really yummy. You know what I mean."

Lettie worried about the Mayor's condition. Maybe she should intervene. But the crowd was loving it. Everyone had soaked up enough airborne mind-altering THC to be fried.

Hope grabbed the mic with both hands. "Wow. Hello Vallejo. I don't know if you are, but I am, well, a little bit ripped. Oh, I don't know."

Rowdy applause came from the spectators.

"I have worked hard to make a success out of today's Re-Sail Fest, and dammit, I've done a great job. And now I'm going to introduce the real Jaylyn Chadwick, and by real, I mean our own living, breathing Vallejo native and college student who blasted into history when El Gordo exploded a month ago. She will be the first customer of our new Mermaid's Flight attraction. After today, the ride will be open to residents and visitors. I must warn you to make reservations, because you know, wink wink, about its reputation for happy endings. Let me tell you…"

Jaylyn stepped up onto the riser next to the Mayor and held both hands aloft. The glowing crowd began waving their upraised hands back and forth in light-headed delight.

The Mayor turned to Jaylyn. "Wow. Are you ready? This will be so awesome."

"I can't wait."

The smoky output from the BigWeed plant had worsened. Dense clouds of white smoke enveloped the festival grounds. The normal cross channel land-scape of defunct warehouses, vacant coal sheds, and abandoned factories became fuzzier. The crowds were fuzzier too.

Jaylyn walked over to the air cannon. There were robust reasons for her to make this flight. The Mayor had promised a full tuition scholarship for the junior and senior years at Brown University. But even more

exciting—this flight could once again trigger the re-
arrangement of her neural connections. An outcome
sure to lead to, well, yum.

She stretched out in the cannon's barrel. RideCo
workers fitted a headset and microphone before closing the Plexiglas cover. A video camera projected her
facial expressions onto an enormous outdoor video
installation. The lower screen readout showed her
pulse and blood pressure. Her heartbeat thumped
rhythmically over the public address system.

The announcer's voice boomed. "Jaylyn, this is
ground control. Are you ready?"

She gave the camera a thumbs up.

The crowd was in hysterics, roaring before raising
their thumbs in response. Some gazed at their thumbs
like they had never seen them before. All were flame-
broiled. Chocolate chip cookie sales skyrocketed.
Strangers were giving each other hugs. Adults spon-
taneously fell down on the lawn laughing, and then
couldn't get up.

The announcer continued. "Ground Control to
brave Jaylyn. Commencing countdown, engines on.
Now, I invite the audience to join me for the countdown."

"Five."

The crowd shrieked. "Four." Two persons standing
at the top of the grandstand waved so hard that they
fell off the back.

The bleachers rocked. "Three."

"Two." The noise was deafening.

"One."

"Ground control to brave Jaylyn. Liftoff."

A thunderous explosive "THUMP" boomed across the Strait and a bright flash and gray cloud billowed out from the launch ramp's stage fireworks. The compressed air cannon worked with perfection and the zoned out crowds witnessed the delighted Jaylyn rising skyward.

She flew headfirst, eyes shut tight, elbows pulled to her torso, tracing an arc like a missile shot into the dense smoky fog over the water. The audience quieted to a level of mild delusion. Jaylyn spread her arms before twirling her hands, sending spooky vortexes spinning away from her fingertips.

The conical swirls generated a collective response. "Oooh."

Then, "Aaah."

Finally, in unison, "Awesome."

The announcer took over. "This is ground control to brave Jaylyn. You've really made the grade."

Her throaty response—strong and clear for all to hear. "Jaylyn to Ground Control. I am floating in a most peculiar way," she reported, "And the Straits look very different today."

The trajectory carried her higher into the mist until the spectators could no longer see her. But her final message boomed from the speakers.

"Yum," she moaned. "Yum and yum. From the ankles. Oh…that…is… yummy."

Epilogue

After Carver Pardon's will had been duly read in a local law office, Maggie and Promise spent days cleaning up their bequest, the forty-two foot Hatteras trawler *Doublecross*. They sold it for close to eighty thousand dollars. Once again half-sisters, each took one-third of the proceeds. A last third they sent to Krista.

Maggie had the local shipyard haul out the *Angry Duck* and begin overdue work on the hull and seals. They also repaired the transmission.

Promise spent her share in Serenity Point, patching up the inside of the levee where the workshop had blown up, rehabbing the spider web of floating docks, and building a sparkling two-stall bathroom next to the Shipwreck. When the new toilets were finished, Promise had the workers construct a triangular river rock base for a monument and a commemorative plaque.

Finally, during a ceremony attended by a dozen people, the participants formed a circle, interlocked hands, and made a commitment to continue a search for world sanity. They stood by for the unveiling of the plaque.

"On this site in Serenity Point, in 1980, a concerned group of scientists and military officers, working in a secret workshop under the code name Mollusk, tried to alter the dangerous course of military nuclear weapon development. Teresa Almeda, Sally Trout, Erika Pazty, Carver Pardon and Lt. René Guillbot created a substitute weapon that used non-lethal elements for its power.

They wanted to call it the Serenity Warhead.
The government hunted these people down but never caught them.

In the end, their efforts for peace failed."

Acknowledgements

Many have helped along the way. I want to thank Annette Blanchard, Tim Blanchard, and the members of the Sausalito Writers Saloon (Chuck Brickley, Scott Seely, and Jennifer Gennari). PR wizard Kaye McKenzie offered comments on the manuscript. Jim Shubin designed the cover and the layout. Ron Jewett is my skilled cartographer. Bill Hewitt and Jerry Hewitt offered many suggestions. Former Vallejo resident and nuclear attack submarine officer Jim Woessner kept the technical details within bounds, and author Gretchen Watkins, a long-time Vallejo resident, was kind enough to check my references to her town and to the old shipyard.

The Author

John Hewitt is a native Californian who now lives north of San Francisco.

He is the author of five offbeat novels celebrating mysterious phenomena in California and Baja California, Mexico.

He has twice been a finalist in the adult fiction humor genre of the Indies national book contest.

97004592R00147

Made in the USA
Columbia, SC
06 June 2018